Aunt Gerda stood in the open doorway. She was wrapped in a gray blanket that trailed on the floor behind her and she had one arm raised, like an Indian chief, or a minister praying.

"Goodnight, Edwin," she called softly.

Edwin? That was the name of one of the dolls.

From outside came a child's voice. "Goodnight, Mother."

What? Who was that? Not Edwin, that was for sure. My legs were weak suddenly and I had to hold on to the wall.

"Goodnight, Fern. Goodnight, George."

Two voices answering, tiny, distant, as if from another planet. "Goodnight, Mother."

THE GHOST CHILDREN

EVE BUNTING

THE GHOST CHILDREN

CLARION BOOKS
New York

Clarion Books
a Houghton Mifflin Company imprint
215 Park Avenue South, New York, NY 10003
Copyright © 1989 by Eve Bunting
First Clarion paperback edition, 2005.

The text was set in 12-point Goudy.

www.houghtonmifflinbooks.com

Printed in the U.S.A.

Library of Congress Cataloging-in-Publication Data

Bunting, Eve, 1928–
The ghost children / Eve Bunting.
p. cm.
Summary: Matt's investigation of vandalism of life-sized dolls
belonging to the strange but well-meaning aunt with whom he
and his sister live takes him to the art world of Los Angeles.
ISBN: 0-89919-843-0
[Mystery and detective stories.] I. Title.
PZ7.B91527 Ghf 1989
[Fic]—dc1988-020356
AC

CL ISBN–13: 978-0-89919-843-9   CL ISBN–10: 0-89919-843-0
PA ISBN–13: 978-0-618-60477-7   PA ISBN–10: 0-618-60477-4

HAD 10 9 8 7 6 5 4 3 2 1

To Margaret Mary Jensen

We've been friends for a long time.

Before . . .

Arabella, Bethlehem, Cleo, Derek, Edwin, Fern, and George stood silently in the dark.

Once Harriette would have been with them, but Harriette was dead and poor Isadora had died before she had lived.

Swaying gently in the night air, Arabella, Bethlehem, Cleo, Derek, Edwin, Fern, and George smiled their painted smiles and watched the road through their sightless eyes.

1

AUNT GERDA wasn't there to meet us when we got off the airport bus at the hotel.

"Where is she, Matt?" Abby asked, clutching her teddy bear, trying to peer through the dark and the rain. "And you and Mrs. Valdoni told me it didn't *rain* in California."

She gave a forlorn hiccup and I put my arm around her and said quickly, "Don't cry. Aunt Gerda will come any minute. It's O.K., Abby." I could feel her sharp little shoulder bones through her wet T-shirt and I edged her under the overhang of the hotel where the airport bus had let us off.

"You go inside the lobby, Abby. I'll wait here."

Abby cringed against me. "I don't want to go any-where. I want to stay with you." I heard the edge of panic in her voice and I squeezed her shoulder again. It must be hard to be five years old, to have no mom, to be in a strange place with only your not-very-big thirteen-year-old brother to keep the scaries away. I was having a problem keeping the scaries away myself. Where *was* Aunt Gerda?

"Well, try to find your jacket and put it on, Ab," I said. "No sense getting pneumonia."

She couldn't open the knot in the strings on her duffel bag, so I gave her Mom's portfolio to hold and did it for her. Her red jacket was on the very bottom. I tried to shake out the wrinkles. "Do you think Aunt Gerda's forgotten we're coming, Matt?" Her eyes were big and scared.

"No way!" I pulled the hood over her straight black hair. "She'll be here any minute."

A gray Cadillac drove in and stopped, and the bellman came pushing through the hotel doors to help the driver with his luggage.

"Don't you kids want to come out of the rain?" the bellman asked.

"We're waiting for our aunt to pick us up."

He nodded. "Well, if she doesn't get here real soon, why don't you come on inside."

"O.K. Thanks." I wiped a smear of wet off the precious portfolio. What if it wasn't waterproof anymore? What if inside it Abby's future and mine were washing away? I pulled a sweatshirt from my bag and wrapped it around the worn plastic. My Seattle Mariners cap tumbled out and I jammed it on my head.

"What time is it, Matt?" Abby asked.

"Ten-thirty."

"Is it ten-thirty back home, too?"

"Yes."

A taxi slid in under the hotel overhang behind the Cadillac and sat with its lights on. I could see the driver behind the beat of the windshield wipers. If Aunt Gerda didn't come in the next half-hour I'd ask him to take us to Sierra Maria Canyon, wherever that was. "My aunt owns the little market there. How much to take us?" I'd ask. There was $138 left after paying Mom's last expenses and our airline tickets from there to here. $138. All we had in the whole world, except the paintings.

A truck was driving in, a pickup, blue and battered and splattered with mud. The driver rolled down the window. "Are you Matt O'Meara?"

"Yes."

"And I'm Abby," my little sister piped up.

"I thought you had to be." The driver was opening the door, jumping down, a tall man wearing a wide cowboy hat and jeans tucked into leather boots. "I'm Slim Ericson. Your aunt asked me to pick you up."

He was grabbing our duffels and smiling down at Abby. "Hi, sweetie! How are you?"

"Fine." Abby took a step toward him, but I held on to her arm.

Mr. Ericson tossed our bags inside the truck. "Sorry I'm late, but when it rains here, drivers go crazy. There was a pile up on Sierra Maria Boulevard that you wouldn't believe and . . ." He stopped. "Aren't you coming? Do you like standing in the rain?"

"No. Ah . . ." I held Abby's arm tightly. All sorts of

thoughts were rushing around in my head. You don't just get in a truck with a strange man even if he does say he knows your aunt. You especially don't let your little sister get into a truck with a strange man. So what if he did know our names?

The man was looking at me, puzzled, and then he pushed back his hat and smiled. I saw the gleam of a gold front tooth. "I get it. You're just being a bit cautious, making sure I am who I say I am. That's good. I've got two kids of my own and I hope they'd be that smart. Well, let's see now. I guess showing you a license wouldn't do any good. How about if I tell you what I know about you? Your Aunt Gerda lives up in the canyon. She's really your great-aunt, your mother's aunt." His voice softened. "Your dad died four years ago and when your mom passed on . . ."

"Went to heaven to be with Daddy," Ab corrected, and Mr. Ericson murmured, "That's right, sweetie. When she went to heaven, too, your Aunt Gerda said you were to come here."

Abby was nodding with that attentive look she gets when someone's reading to her or telling her a bedtime story.

"Aunt Gerda's the only family we've got," she said. "Mom told us."

"So I hear." Mr. Ericson touched Abby's cheek with a stubby finger. "Your mom was an artist, a painter . . ."

It was my turn to interrupt. "A *great* painter," I said and Mr. Ericson nodded.

"Your Aunt Gerda has one of her pictures hanging

right there in her living room, one of a house and the ocean, kind of misty."

I pushed Abby forward. "It's O.K. to get in now. Thanks for coming for us, Mr. Ericson."

"My pleasure. Gerda didn't want to leave the children."

"Children?" What was he talking about? What children?

Abby was sliding into the truck, bumping herself across the wide front seat, but I paused, part in, part out.

"I don't understand," I said. "Aunt Gerda doesn't *have* children. Does she babysit, or what?"

"She hasn't told you about them?"

"No."

Rain ran off the brim of his hat in a steady stream.

"Well, the children aren't alive. They're . . ."

From inside the truck came a scared little voice. "You mean there are dead children at Aunt Gerda's? You mean, dead . . . like Mom?"

"No, no, sweetie," Mr. Ericson said. "Nothing like that. Wrong choice of words. I mean, they're not real, that's all. Gerda imagines they are . . ." I sensed him fumbling for words. "It would be better if she tells you about them herself. It's too hard to explain. Climb in, Matt. You're getting soaked."

I got in, slammed the door behind me, and in a few seconds we were whizzing through city streets, rain rushing down the gutters on either side, cars meeting us in a dazzle of headlights.

Mr. Ericson nodded down at the portfolio. "Do you have your mom's drawings in there?"

"Some of them," I said. "We left most of them with our neighbor in Seattle."

"Mrs. Valdoni," Abby said. "She's our friend. Matt says if it's awful here maybe we can . . ."

"Shh, Ab. You aren't supposed to blab about that, remember? It would hurt Aunt Gerda, and besides . . ."

Abby nodded and put her thumb in her mouth. No use finishing that "besides." Mrs. Valdoni had only a two-bedroom apartment for Mr. Valdoni and her and their five kids.

I peered at the shining street ahead and thought about our Aunt Gerda, the one we knew about but had never met. What was this about imaginary children? People who live alone get weird sometimes. I understood that. And it had been three years since Uncle Joseph had died. But in her letters Aunt Gerda sounded fine. "Your mother was very dear to us. When your neighbor called, I knew your home from now on should be here with me."

She'd sounded nice. Mrs. Valdoni had thought so, too. And there'd been her letters when Mom was alive. Mom had read them to us, all of them filled with love and caring. Aunt Gerda had sent money sometimes, when things were hardest for us. Mom had told us stories about how wonderful she and Uncle Joseph had been when Mom was young, when she'd gone to spend vacations with them. It would be all right. Mom would never have told Mrs. Valdoni to

6

get in touch with Aunt Gerda for us if it wasn't all right. Mom had loved us so much. I blinked and swallowed.

Ab had fallen asleep with her head on my chest, the way she'd done on the plane. I moved a little to make her more comfortable. "Take care of your baby sister, Matt," Mom had said, just before she died.

"I will, Mom. I will."

We were driving through a small village with one narrow street now. Then we turned left on a dirt road, gravel sputtering from under our wheels.

"This is the start of the canyon," Mr. Ericson said. "Home to artists, rock hounds, nature lovers. And old-timers." He pointed. "That there's the Greeley house." The headlights picked up a small cabin. "Clay Greeley's about your age, but he hasn't too many friends."

I'd had friends in Seattle. John Estevez and Blinky Irvine and Knock Knock Silverstein. We called him "Knock Knock" because he was all the time asking goofy knock knock jokes. Knock Knock said he'd write if he heard a good new one. They'd all said they'd miss me.

Mr. Ericson glanced at me sideways. "Mostly the canyon kids are scared of Clay Greeley. Not my Kristin, though. My Kristin's not afraid of anything."

I didn't answer, but I was thinking, What's so great about that? What does his Kristin have to be afraid of? She has a nice dad, and probably a nice mom, and a home, and enough to eat, and no worries. She didn't have to leave her friends and come to a strange, new place. I wouldn't be afraid of anything either if I were Kristin.

Three figures were walking on the road in front of us and Mr. Ericson slowed. Boys, I thought, all of them wearing slick rain ponchos, each of them carrying a heavy-looking white plastic grocery sack.

They glanced back as Mr. Ericson sounded the horn and moved to walk in a single file.

"That's Clay Greeley now," Mr. Ericson said, passing carefully. "And Castor and Pollux, the twins. They're just about his only buddies. People around here call them the heavenly twins because of their names, but don't be fooled. There's nothing heavenly about either of them. I wonder where they're heading and what they're up to on a night like this? Nothing good, whatever it is."

Teddy had slipped off Ab's lap and I bent to pick him up without disturbing her.

"You must be tired, too, Matt," Mr. Ericson said gently. "Hang in there. It won't be much longer."

I closed my eyes for a couple of minutes, then opened them again as I felt the truck slow and stop.

"Here's your new home," Mr. Ericson said, and I sat, holding Teddy, my arm still around Ab, staring at the house that was going to be our home.

It was faded and white, square and wooden, and it tilted drunkenly to one side. Every window had a light in it, as if to welcome us. A spotlight at the front shone on slick metal signs stuck in the front grass. "DRINK COCA-COLA." "MORTON'S SALT." Pieces of soggy cardboard dripped from the trees. "HOMEMADE SANDWICHES SERVED HERE." "WE HAVE POP ON ICE, BUT WHERE THE HECK IS MOM?"

"Abby." I shook her shoulder gently. "Wake up, Ab. We're here."

When I opened the door, cool air wafted in. The rain was over, but I heard it rustling in the trees, heard the noisy chorus of crickets, which stopped, then started again. I eased my wet jeans from my knees, took Mom's portfolio, and jumped down. Abby held on to my shoulder and climbed out beside me, clutching Teddy. My legs were weak and shaky. This was it, then. The end of the line.

A bare yellow bulb shone on the porch, lighting up two rattan rockers and a table with a book propped under one leg. The patch of grass beyond the path lay in darkness, out of reach of the spotlight, but I sensed something there, some things. What was that whispering, breathing sound? I peered into the shadows, my skin prickling. There were figures there, swaying slightly. There were lumpy, shapeless bodies.

Instinctively, I stepped back, tripping over Abby.

"Who are those people?" she asked, her voice too high, filled with fear.

"I don't know." I turned, to shield her, to edge her back toward the truck.

"It's all right." Mr. Ericson stood on the path behind us, holding our two bags. "No need to be scared. Those are the children."

2

THAT TALL, broad woman opening the front door now must be Aunt Gerda. I turned, feeling the drag of Abby's little hands on the back of my jacket.

"Loosen up, Ab," I muttered. "You're strangling me."

"We're here, Gerda," Slim Ericson called. "Half-drowned, but otherwise safe and sound."

I couldn't see Aunt Gerda's face, only the gray shine of her hair and her large bulky outline that almost filled the doorway. I could see the way she held out her arms in welcome and hear the warmth in her voice as she called:

"Matthew! Abigail! You poor dears. You must be worn out. And me not there to tell you how glad I am that you've come."

Mr. Ericson was trying to urge us forward, but Abby had her feet stubbornly planted and wouldn't move. Fear rose from her like steam. I turned my head sideways, just a little. The light from the open door fell in a white block across the grass, picking up one of the figures as if in a spotlight.

It was a doll. Just a girl doll, life-sized, with a smooth, brightly painted face. She wore an old-fashioned pink dress with a wet droopy frill around the bottom, white stockings, black shoes. I could see other dolls, too, a shadowy group of them, all huddled together on the grass.

The girl doll turned toward the porch and as if on a signal the others turned, too. My skin prickled. They could *move?* And then I saw that each one stood on a big wooden thing, like a turntable. Criminy! That had been scary for a minute, all right.

"They're just dolls," I whispered to Abby. "Nothing to worry about."

Aunt Gerda was coming down the steps now, putting an arm around each of us.

"I'm so happy to have you. Thank you for bringing them, Slim. What would I have done without you? You'll come in, too, for a few minutes?"

"Thanks, Gerda, but I have to be off," Mr. Ericson said. "I'll just put these bags inside."

He was behind us as we went up the steps and onto the porch.

"Do the children look all right?" Aunt Gerda asked Mr. Ericson, and for a minute I thought she was talking about Ab and me. But she wasn't. I saw that she was peering past us into the darkness, to the grass beyond the house lights where the dolls stood.

"They look just fine to me, Gerda," Mr. Ericson said gently.

"I don't like them to be out in the rain like this," Aunt Gerda said. "It worries me. I really should have tried to get them all in before it started."

"It won't do them any harm, Gerda. You fuss about them too much." Mr. Ericson set our duffels by the bottom of a flight of stairs that ran up from the living room.

"Well, now," Aunt Gerda said. "Let me look at you two! Abigail, you are so pretty. You're just like your mother when she was your age . . . those lovely dark eyes, that hair . . . and Matthew!" She smiled down at me. I could tell she'd had big dark eyes once herself, but they had faded to a pale, pale brown. There was nothing faded about her smile. "Your mother wrote so much about you, Matthew. You were her Rock of Gibraltar, she said. Her strong, wise, capable son."

She knelt in front of us and Abby hung back at first, then swayed forward to hug her, to snuggle tight against her neck. Aunt Gerda smoothed Abby's hair and said, "There, there. Everything's going to be all right, my dear." And suddenly I believed her. We were wanted, we were welcome. It *was* going to be all right.

Over Aunt Gerda's shoulder I saw Slim Ericson wave to me and mouth "So long" as he let himself out the front door, and then a slight movement somewhere else in the room made me look in that direction. One of the big dolls stood in the middle of the room. He had silvery hair, spun like candy floss, and he seemed to be getting fitted for a new jacket. His pants were black-and-white checked. He wore a white T-shirt with a mended tear across the front and half of a black blazer and he was looking straight at me and smiling. That smile turned my bones to mush. How could he be so real looking? How could the skin on his face be so smooth and fleshy? Of course it wasn't skin. But what was it?

I shivered and Aunt Gerda turned to look where I was looking.

"Oh, Matthew, Abigail, this is Derek. Derek stands closest to the road and somebody threw paint on him. It got all over his front, but I found him some new pants and pretty soon he's going to have a new jacket, aren't you, Derek?"

"Is he a doll?" Abby asked, standing and taking an uncertain step toward him. For some reason I wanted to reach out and jerk her back.

Aunt Gerda lowered her voice. "Don't ever let him hear you ask that, Abigail. He's very sensitive about what we call him."

Abby was smiling and nodding now and I could tell she thought this was a neat game, the kind of "Let's pretend" she really liked.

"Hello, Derek," she said.

"I wouldn't be surprised if Derek got that paint on himself on purpose," Aunt Gerda whispered. "He never did like the nice green pants and jacket he had before. Derek is our picky one."

Now Abby was giggling. "Picky Derek!"

"Abby!" I hadn't meant to say her name so sharply. "Why don't you grab your bag and Aunt Gerda can show us where we're going to sleep. Abby's real tired," I told Aunt Gerda.

"Of course. What am I thinking of? There'll be lots of time for you to get acquainted with Derek and the others. I'll show you your room. Here, Matthew. Let me carry something for you."

I let her take Mom's portfolio and I picked up the two bags and followed her and Abby up stairs that were steep and narrow, each step sloping to the right. It was like being on board a tilting ship. I wondered if there'd been an earthquake since the house was built or if it had just gotten tired of standing straight. It had to be really old. I glanced back over my shoulder into the room below and for the first time I saw that it was part shop, part living room, part kitchen. For the first time, too, I saw what kept Derek upright. He wasn't on a turntable after all.

A long wooden pole went under his clothes in back and came up behind his neck. Its end was fitted into the center hole of the round wooden platform he stood on. The platform was as big as an automobile tire but shaped like a spool of thread. From here, it looked as if Derek had three legs, his own two in the black checked pants and a third in between. The pole, loose in its setting, moved easily and he moved with it.

In front of me Abby was chattering to Aunt Gerda. "Do you have any girl dolls?"

"Indeed. We have three girls. Three girls and four boys. Your uncle made them all for me and named them alphabetically. We have Arabella. She's our eldest. We have Bethlehem, Cleo, Derek, whom you've met. Then we have Edwin, Fern, and George. Quite a little family. We did have another girl, Harriette, but we lost her."

"Can I play with Arabella and George and . . . and the rest of them?" Ab asked.

"They're looking forward to it," Aunt Gerda said. "I've told them all about you."

"Maybe we could have a tea party and my teddy could come?" Abby suggested. Mrs. Valdoni and Abby and Teddy had had lots of tea parties in Seattle. I hadn't minded those. But I didn't like the thought of this one.

"They love tea parties," Aunt Gerda said and I felt cold and clammy. There was something not right about the way Aunt Gerda talked about these dolls. "They're not real, but Gerda imagines they are," Mr. Ericson had said. Oh, brother! What *was* this? Was she crazy? I'd have to try explaining to Ab that she shouldn't start thinking about dolls the way Aunt Gerda did, as if they were alive. But I'd have to be careful not to scare her. Real careful.

Aunt Gerda threw open a door. "Here we are."

The light was already on inside the room and I saw a single bed with a white tufted spread, a scarred dresser that had rows of little drawers and a spotted mirror, and a big plump chair. A folding cot with a

15

faded blue cover had been placed right next to the bed. On the floor was a rug made up of blue, white, and red circles that went around in an endless braid. On the wall was a painting my mom had done, the one Slim Ericson had told us about.

I stood looking up at it, and Aunt Gerda put the portfolio on the bed and came to stand beside me.

"I had that in the living room downstairs where I could see it all the time. But I thought you should have it up here, to bring her close to you."

My throat had gone dry, my eyes stung. Clear as clear could be, I remembered my mother standing in front of her easel, her head cocked, the old shirt she wore covered with streaks of paint. I saw her face when she turned to me, eyes shining.

"What do you think, Matt? Did I get it? Is that the way the sun looks on the water? Oh, how I wish I were better at this! It's all here, behind my eyes. But does it come out right? Is that the way you see it?"

I clenched my fists around the strings of the two duffels. Mom! Mom!

"My mama did that," Abby said, looking up at the painting, nodding her head. "My mama was a terrific artist, Matt says."

"Yes, she was." Aunt Gerda's voice was soft. "This was her room when she was a little girl and stayed with us. I have another bedroom, Abigail, and that can be yours if you want it. But for now I thought you might like to be here with Matthew. You and I can start fixing up the other room. We can put new wallpaper on and you can help me make curtains."

Abby moved closer to me. "Can I just stay with Matt all the time?"

"If that's what you want, my dear. Now the bathroom's right next door. If you're too tired to take a bath tonight, leave it till morning. Come down when you're ready. You must be hungry after your trip."

"Thanks," I said. "Are you hungry, Ab?"

Ab nodded.

"I am, too," I told Aunt Gerda. "But getting clean might be a good idea."

"I've left out towels," Aunt Gerda said.

As soon as she left, I went into the bathroom and ran water into the big claw-footed tub.

"And don't just sit in it and play," I told Ab. "Wash!"

While she was gone, I took my sweatshirt from around the portfolio and spread the paintings on the bed. They were all dry. The one of Abby and me, Ab in her little shorts and striped T-shirt gathering pebbles on the beach, me with my kite; the one with the ferry on its way to Orcas, the blue green of the water flecked with foam; the self-portrait of Mom. She'd been pretty sick when she did that and you could see her bones through her skin. I looked at it for a long time before I put it back. How could we bear to part with a single one? Because we had to, that's how.

When Ab came back, I took my bath, wallowing in the water, trying to let the worries go. Too soon to worry anyway. And silly. I should just be glad we had somewhere to go, someone to take us.

Ab was already in her yellow nightgown when I came out of the bathroom. She was sitting cross-legged in the middle of the bed, Teddy with his head on the pillow.

"I see you've taken the bed, brat," I told her, drying the ends of her hair with a towel. "I thought you were hungry. Don't you want to go down and eat?"

"Yeah," Abby said, but she didn't move and I saw her yawn.

"How about if I go ask Aunt Gerda if I can bring something up for you?"

"No. No, Matty." She was scrambling off the bed, catching her toes in the hem of the nightgown, her eyes wide and frightened. "Don't leave me."

"Take it easy, Ab. I won't leave you. We'll both . . ."

And then there was a knock and Aunt Gerda came in with a tray. "I thought this might be easier tonight," she said. There were two bowls of soup and a plate of bread and two glasses of milk on the tray.

She put it on the dresser and I pulled over the chair so Abby could kneel and eat right there while I sat on the end of the cot.

"Tomorrow you can see everything," Aunt Gerda said. "The Ericson children will probably come over. Kristin does, most days, and sometimes her little brother comes, too." She picked up a brush from the dresser and began to brush Ab's hair.

"And can we have a tea party?" Ab asked.

"Abby," I said. "Don't talk with your mouth full."

Aunt Gerda smiled. "I'll tell the children about the tea party when I go back downstairs. That way they can look forward to it."

I kept my head bent finishing my soup.

"All done?" Aunt Gerda asked, taking my empty bowl, putting it with Abby's on the tray.

"It was great," I said. "Thanks."

"You're welcome." She drew the blue curtains closed. "Into bed now, Abigail. You too, Matthew."

"Can't I carry the tray downstairs for you?"

"I'm perfectly able to do that myself. But thank you for offering."

I waited until Ab got between the sheets, then tucked her in. "Goodnight. God bless," I said the way Mom always used to say, the way I'd said every night since she died.

"Goodnight, Matty." Abby held her face off the pillow so I could more easily kiss her cheek.

I wriggled myself into the squeaky cot.

"And who's going to tuck you in, you big, capable boy?" Aunt Gerda said softly. She came over, smoothed my sheet, touched my face. "Goodnight and God bless. And you, dear little Abigail."

I watched as she took the tray and carried it to the door. "Can you get the light, Matthew?" she asked.

I nodded.

"Sleep well."

I clicked off the lamp and listened to her footsteps going downstairs.

"Matt?" Abby whispered. "Are you there?"

"Of course I'm here, goose. Put out your hand."

I took it and held it tight.

"She's nice, isn't she, Matt?"

"Real nice," I said. And I did think she was nice—weird but nice.

Soon I felt Abby's hand go limp and heard her little snoring sounds start. Through the darkness I tried to see my mother's painting, but I couldn't. It was good, though, to know it was there. Tomorrow I'd take some others from the portfolio and prop them up where we could see them, too.

I don't know if I went to sleep and if it was the small squeak of the screen door downstairs that wakened me. Maybe I was awake already. Ab's hand had slipped from mine.

In the room below, someone was talking.

Aunt Gerda, talking to herself? Or to Derek? But weren't there two voices? Someone must have come calling.

I got out of the cot, tiptoed to the door, and eased it open.

The stairs were flooded with light, and so were the living room/shop downstairs and the outside porch.

Aunt Gerda stood in the open doorway. She was wrapped in a gray blanket that trailed on the floor behind her and she had one arm raised, like an Indian chief, or a minister praying.

"Goodnight, Edwin," she called softly.

Edwin? That was the name of one of the dolls.

From outside came a child's voice. "Goodnight, Mother."

What? Who was that? Not Edwin, that was for sure. My legs were weak suddenly and I had to hold on to the wall.

"Goodnight, Fern. Goodnight, George."

Two voices answering, tiny, distant, as if from another planet. "Goodnight, Mother."

I stepped back, closed the bedroom door, and leaned against it, my heart pounding. Then I crept back onto the cot as close to my baby sister as I could get, and lay there, shivering in the dark.

3

I SLEPT late, and it was Abby who woke me, tugging at my nose, bouncing on my cot till it squeaked and creaked.

"Wake up, Matt. Wake up." She had already opened the curtains and the room was filled with sunlight.

I groaned and put my arms across my eyes.

"Come on, Matt. I have something to show you. It's outside, out in Aunt Gerda's garden, but you can see it from the window."

I was coming awake now, remembering Aunt Gerda and where we were, remembering the dolls and the way they'd said goodnight. The cold feeling came slithering back inside me. I bit my knuckles. They couldn't have talked. I'd been dreaming. Or else Aunt Gerda had called goodnight into the garden and then answered herself in a tiny doll voice. Sure! Abby did that all the time.

"Do you want to go for a walk, Teddy?" she'd ask.

"Oh, yes, please, Mommy Abby." That was supposed to be Teddy.

Now I let her pull me up, then get behind and make train noises as she pushed me over to the window. Abby hadn't sounded this chipper in a long time. I could tell she was beginning to feel safe here. She was, but I wasn't.

"Look!" She pointed outside.

The rain had disappeared as if it had never been and the morning sparkled. Beneath the window was an overgrown vegetable garden and a shed with a sloping roof.

"Down there, Matt," Abby said. "You're not looking in the right place."

Now I saw a swing hanging from the branch of an old tree. The seat sloped at one end and moved a little in the breeze.

"A swing, Matt. Can I try it?"

"We'll see," I said.

Abby's hair spiked in all directions and there was stuff in the corners of her eyes.

"First, go wash and put your clothes on," I said. "Match things up the way Mom taught you. Then we can go downstairs."

"Yippee." She began pulling a tangle of pants and shirts from her duffel.

I turned to stare out the window again while she got dressed. Sometimes I thought how much easier it would have been if I'd had a little brother instead of a little sister. He and I could have horsed around in our

23

underwear even. With a little sister I had to be polite. Still, I knew I wouldn't trade Ab for anybody in the whole world, not anybody.

What was that?

I stood high on my toes. There was something else down there, way back in the corner behind the swing. I stretched, putting my face close to the glass. It was a wooded cross, white, newly painted. A grave! Whose?

"Matt?" Abby held a pair of rolled together yellow socks. "Do these match these?" She arched her back and stuck out her stomach so I could see her blue shorts and her blue and yellow striped T-shirt.

"They'll look great, Ab," I said. "Good job."

How could I fix it that she wouldn't see that grave and remember two other graves, the two crosses that marked them? I couldn't. I couldn't protect her from remembering.

While she washed, I dressed, and then she waited for me. We helped each other make the bed and cot.

"Matt? You won't let Aunt Gerda put me in a room by myself, will you?"

"I won't, Ab. But you have to promise not to pull my nose in the morning."

"Can I pull your hair? You're hard to wake up."

"No. Not my hair either. Are you ready? Let's go."

"Can I see Mama's picture first?"

"Sure." I opened the portfolio, found the self-portrait, and propped it on the dresser. Mama smiled out at us. I wondered how long it would take for the ache that came when I looked at her to stop. Maybe it never would.

"We can keep this here if you like, Ab. Do you want to?"

Abby nodded. Her shoulders dropped and her face looked awfully small as she stared up at me. "Matt? Tell me again what we're going to do."

I sat on the edge of the cot and she sat, too, and I put my arm around her shoulder and squeezed her tight.

"Well, as soon as I can I'm going to find an art dealer, a really big, important one. We'll keep some of the pictures for ourselves . . ."

"The one of Mom, and the one of me and you, and the one of Tetley," Abby said.

"Yes." Tetley was Mrs. Valdoni's dog. "Those. Whatever we want. The rest we'll sell. We'll get thousands and thousands of dollars and we'll . . ."

Abby interrupted, her eyes on my face. "You said thousands and thousands and thousands before, Matt. You forgot one."

"Thousands and thousands and thousands," I agreed. "A lot. We'll tell the guy who buys them that first we want to show them in a big gallery—an exhibit, it's called. That way everyone will be able to see Mom's work and admire it. She'd like that. And then he'll give us the money, and we'll put it in a bank, and it will be ours so we don't have to depend on anyone but each other."

"And we'll buy a house . . ." Abby had her wide-eyed, story-listening look again.

"We'll buy a house . . ."

"And get a kitty cat . . . and live happily ever after." Abby finished with a sigh of satisfaction.

"Right."

I knew it wouldn't be this simple or easy, but I knew, too, that the paintings were our legacy from Mom and that this was what she would have wanted for Ab and me as soon as we got things together.

"Maybe we'll like it here and stay forever and give Aunt Gerda the money," Abby said.

"Maybe." I sort of doubted it. We went downstairs.

The living room/kitchen/shop was empty, except for Derek, who still stood on the platform, wearing his unfinished jacket. Sun streamed through the screen door where Aunt Gerda stood last night in her trailing blanket. Or where I'd dreamed I'd seen her stand last night . . .

"I like this little house," Abby said, clutching Teddy and jumping down the last two steps of the stairs. It kills me the way Abby jumps, with her feet together and her knees bent and her mouth set in this little tight line as she concentrates. You'd think she was in the Olympics or something.

"Hi, Derek," she said. "Have you had breakfast?" And then she ran past him, "Oh, look, Matt. I can play shop in here for real."

"No kidding." I followed her across to the long wooden counter at the front end of the room, being careful not to look at Derek. Underneath the counter were glass cases that held packets of sugar and faded boxes of cereal and dusty cans of soup. There was lots of space behind the glass, lots of emptiness. Aunt Gerda didn't keep a big stock, but it looked as if she kept what she had for a long time.

A big white freezer chest against the wall hummed up a storm. At the kitchen end were a stove and a sink and cupboards painted blue. There was a couch on the other side, several big wicker baskets, a sewing machine. The walls were of rough paneling, painted white, and the ceiling was low and paneled, too. By the front door was an old-fashioned trunk, banded in metal, and above the counter a framed picture of President Kennedy and a clock with OVALTINE printed around its face.

"Aunt Gerda?" Abby called, running across to the screen door. Her voice was as high as a bird's.

From outside came an answering call. "Abigail? Matthew? I'm out here, with the children."

Abby turned her shining face up to me. "Now we'll get to meet the other dolls."

Great, I thought. I took hold of her arm. "Listen a minute, Ab. Aunt Gerda is very old. She's even older than our grandmother would be if we had a grand-mother. She thinks those dolls are real . . . remember, Mr. Ericson told us? I don't want you to believe her." It bothered me that Derek was listening to this. But of course he wasn't. Not really.

"Oh, Matty!" Abby looked sorry for me. "You are

27

so silly. I know they're not real. That's just Aunt Gerda's pretend. She's just *playing*. Come on!"

"Quit pulling at me," I said. "You're all the time pushing or shoving me. I've got legs, you know. I can walk by myself." I opened the screen door.

Abby danced ahead, Teddy safely tucked against her chest, but I followed more slowly. What was *my* problem? Abby knew the dolls weren't real. Did I think they were? Of course not. That had just been Aunt Gerda talking to herself last night. So why was I so scared of them?

Aunt Gerda stood on the grass with the dolls swaying gently around her. I saw that they moved easily on their poles in those center holes. All it took was a little puff of wind. See? I told myself. Last night you thought they could move by themselves! You thought they could talk *and* move. See?

A stronger little whisk of wind rustled the metal signs and made the cardboard pieces flap against the trees. The dolls swung slowly to face us and Abby gasped and held Teddy up to cover her eyes. She spoke around him.

"Oh, Aunt Gerda," she said in a heartbroken voice. "What happened? What happened to your dollies?"

4

THE DOLLS were covered from head to toe with blobs of purple paint. I took a step closer. No, not paint, something sticky and mushy . . . and not covered head to toe, either. All their faces were clean, spared somehow or washed already by Aunt Gerda.

"Oh, criminy, that's awful," I said. "What *is* that stuff on them?"

Aunt Gerda's face was grim. "Plums. Ripe plums." She pushed back her hair, which was hanging, gray and wispy around her shoulders, and gestured toward the road. "Someone stood there and threw them."

Someone with good aim, I thought. Or someone who came all the way in here, so close it was impossible to miss.

"That's mean." Abby ran forward to take Aunt Gerda's hand. "Why would anyone do such a mean thing?"

"I'm afraid not everyone around here likes me, or

the children," Aunt Gerda said. "A few things have been happening. We had a . . ." She stopped and I had a definite feeling that whatever she'd been going to say had been scary, too scary to tell us about. "A few days ago Derek had that paint thrown on him," she went on. "Now this." She stroked Ab's hair. "Don't worry about it, my dear. We'll get the children cleaned up."

"Is that why you don't like to leave them?" Abby asked, looking at her. "Is that why you didn't come to meet us?"

"Yes. I watch over them very carefully, but we're all so vulnerable at night. I wish I could afford to put up a high fence and a gate and . . ."

"When we get our picture money," Abby began and then glanced guiltily at me. Aunt Gerda hadn't seemed to notice.

I looked more closely at the dolls. What a mess. How in the world would she ever get them cleaned up? And they were so weird; no wonder not everybody liked them. I wasn't too crazy about them myself. Although they were probably uglier today than ever with plum pulp stuck on them, they'd be ugly at any time. The painted eyes on their wooden faces were too far apart, so that each eye seemed to look in a different direction. And why were they all smiling? Couldn't one or two of them have had different expressions? At least?

They were like sextuplets, or whatever you call seven of a kind. Only their fake-looking hair and their clothes were different. I'd never seen such clothes. They could have come out of a museum. All of the girls had purses and jewelry, and one wore a red felt hat with a wet feather in it on her yarn curls. I tried not to shiver.

Something blew against my leg and I bent to pull it off. It was a white plastic grocery bag. Right away I remembered the three figures walking single file along the road last night.

"Clay Greeley," Mr. Ericson had said. And his two friends, somebody and somebody. I'd forgotten their names. The heavenly twins.

I opened the sack and peered inside. Half of a rotten plum was squashed on the bottom. But it was silly to jump to conclusions. These bags were used in just about every market. There must be millions of them around. No need to think this was the "nothing good" Clay and his friends had been up to.

"Yucko!" Abby lifted one foot. A plum oozed on the sole of her shoe, the stain spreading up onto the white top. She came hopping toward me, Aunt Gerda following behind.

"I'm just sorry this had to happen on your first day here," Aunt Gerda said and stopped. She lifted a hand to shield her eyes from the sun, looking beyond us in the direction of the road.

"Well," she said dryly. "Here come the vigilantes."

"Vigilantes?" I turned in time to see two cars pull up and stop on the other side of the road, across from the house. A woman and three men got out of the first car and two more men and a woman joined them from the second. There was something purposeful and a little scary about the way they marched, in double file up the path.

"They're not really vigilantes," Aunt Gerda said in a voice that she seemed to be making loud on purpose, so they'd be sure to hear. "It's just that they act as if they were."

"What's a viggie lantern?" Abby whispered to me, and Aunt Gerda said: "A person who takes the law into his own hands, Abigail."

Abby gave me a glance more puzzled than ever and I wasn't sure I knew myself.

The seven of them had stopped a few feet away from us and one man stepped out in front of the group. He was about Mr. Ericson's age, nice enough looking, with hair dark and straight as Abby's. He wore a tweed sports coat with elbow patches, cords, and comfortable, worn loafers.

"Good morning, Mrs. Yourra," he said.

"Good morning, Mr. Terlock." Aunt Gerda made a funny little bow in his direction and another toward the people on the path.

"I see someone paid you a visit during the night." Mr. Terlock gestured at the dolls, who turned on their poles as if to include everyone in their painted smiles.

"A rather unpleasant visit," Aunt Gerda said.

"I'm sorry, Mrs. Yourra, but I can't say I'm surprised," Mr. Terlock said. "You know very well how the canyon people feel about your dolls. Unpleasantness is bound to occur."

Abby tugged on my arm and I bent toward her. "I don't see anything in their hands," she whispered. "Aunt Gerda said they had the law in their hands. Where is it?"

"I'll explain later," I whispered back, straightening, anxious not to miss a word of what was going on.

"I'm presuming none of you had anything to do with this particular nastiness." I couldn't tell if Aunt Gerda meant it or if she was being sarcastic.

"I promise you we did not," Mr. Terlock said. "This kind of thing is not our style."

There was a mixed chorus of "Certainly nots" from the group on the path. One of the women spoke: "You're lucky it wasn't anything worse, Gerda."

"I've already had worse, Violet," Aunt Gerda said.

"Who are these two young people?" the other woman asked. She was young with a sharp, pointy face. She wore a plaid jacket and jeans that were tucked into tall leather boots.

"They're relatives of mine. They've come to live here," Aunt Gerda said, moving a step closer to Ab and me and putting her arms around our shoulders.

"They're going to be living *here*?" The sharp, pointy-faced woman had a sharp, pointy voice to match.

"Yes," I said. "From now on."

"All the more reason to listen to us, Gerda," Mr. Terlock said. "We've come again to try to convince you to get rid of the dolls. You've lived in peace in this canyon for a lot of years. The trouble only started when you and Joseph insisted on putting these . . . these . . ." His hand swept again toward the dolls. "Making these dolls and displaying them outside."

"I will not get rid of my children, Mr. Terlock," Aunt Gerda said in a voice so fierce that I could hardly believe it when Mr. Terlock smiled. "I will not get rid of them no matter how many times you ask."

"They are not children, my dear Gerda."

The woman, Violet, interrupted. "They're idols. Heathen idols."

"Whatever they are, they are ugly and frightening," Mr. Terlock went on. People have to live in this canyon. *We* have to live here."

"And you have to sell property here, Mr. Terlock. I understand completely," Aunt Gerda said.

"Yes, I do have to sell property here. This is a desirable area." He gestured up and down the road. "But you and your dolls do not do anything to improve land values. I had a couple just last week who wanted to buy up at Tor Peak. When they drove past here, the lady asked if you kept these carvings out here all the time and I had to say 'yes,' Mrs. Yourra. They didn't buy."

"You yourself don't mind, though, do you, Mr. Terlock?" Aunt Gerda asked. "I hear you've bought the old Paterson place and the Jennings ranch."

"That has nothing to do with why we're here," another man said. "My kids have to pass this house on their way to school. Their mother has to drive them. They won't come on their own."

"I'm sorry to hear that," Aunt Gerda said. "But who is filling their minds with fear? Not I, certainly. We would never harm them. If they want to come by, I'll introduce them to the children. They can see for themselves how friendly we are."

The man gave a disbelieving bark of a laugh. "Oh, sure."

"This is my property," Aunt Gerda said. "I will keep my children with me, and I will keep them wherever I want to keep them. There is nothing that says I have to do otherwise. If there was a law, you would have already found it."

"Would you consider moving elsewhere?" Mr. Terlock asked. "I would be willing to give you a fair market value for your home here."

"My home is not for sale," Aunt Gerda said. "And now if you will excuse me." She made that polite little bow again, then stood, stern and proud.

Mr. Terlock said, "I think you will be sorry." What funny lips he had, so thin and pale that they were almost invisible. Like lizard lips.

Aunt Gerda's shoulder stiffened. "Is that some kind of a threat? I don't take easily to threats."

Mr. Terlock didn't answer. Instead, he pushed his way through the group and led them again, back down the path. We stood silently, till the two cars swung around on the narrow road, turned, and roared away.

"Are they bad people?" Abby looked anxiously from me to Aunt Gerda.

"Probably not," Aunt Gerda said. "They just want what they want. And they don't much care how they get it. Now," she turned toward the dolls, "let's think about something important. I'm afraid all of the children's clothes will have to be washed. Some of them may even be ruined completely."

"I'll help." Abby smoothed her hand back and forth along Aunt Gerda's arm. "Don't worry. I'm a good washer."

"Thank you, dear. We'll have to bring them inside, though. I can't possibly embarrass them by undressing them out here."

Another white bag had wrapped itself around the base of a tree. I picked my way through the plum-pocked grass and pulled it free, rolled it up, and pushed it inside the first one. I didn't see a third bag, but if there was such a thing it could have blown any-where. And anyway, I wasn't so sure anymore that Clay Greeley and his friends were the ones who'd messed up the dolls.

"We'll bring the children in one by one," Aunt Gerda said. "Now, let's see. Fern! I know how impor-tant it is to you to look nice. You will be first."

She took Fern around the waist and lifted her up, straight out of the platform.

I thrust the plastic bags at Ab. "Hold these, Ab. Aunt Gerda, I'll carry the doll."

"It's perfectly all right, Matthew. I'm strong. And I'm used to this," Aunt Gerda said, but I grabbed Fern around the waist and Aunt Gerda let her go.

Man, was Fern heavy! Heavier than Abby. She swayed dangerously and I set the pole on the grass to get a better hold of her, then took her again and began walking. She felt hard and solid. What had I suspected? Suppose, when I put my arms around her, she'd been soft and squishy in the middle, like a person? What if I'd heard her stomach gurgle?

Baloney! Double baloney!

I staggered with Fern up the path, Aunt Gerda and Abby behind.

"Get the screen door for me, Ab," I puffed. "But don't come in with that gucky shoe."

"I'll just get the platform for Fern so she can stand," Aunt Gerda said, passing me. "I keep some spares on the service porch. That way I don't have to haul one in from the yard every time I need it."

I leaned Fern against the counter. Her stubby legs in their white, spattered stockings were shorter than the center pole and she began to tilt sideways. I got her in time. Her left eye watched me and she smiled with delight. The opening of the screen door must have been enough to move Derek because he had turned to face us. "You quit grinning," I told Fern. "And you, Derek, don't you be so nosy."

Oh, no! I'd started talking to the dumb dolls, too. But they were so lifelike! I thought of the children who had to be driven to school because they were afraid to walk past them. Not much wonder.

Aunt Gerda came through the back door from the service porch then, wheeling one of the big spools.

Together she and I eased Fern's pole into the platform. It was like putting a patio umbrella into its stand, except that a patio umbrella doesn't smile and wink at you. Wink? Of course Fern hadn't winked. I'd probably blinked, that was all.

"There now," Aunt Gerda said with satisfaction. "We'll get you out of these messy clothes now, Fern, and you'll feel better."

Abby came padding across the room in her yellow socks.

"Should I take off Fern's shoes, too?" she asked, and Aunt Gerda said: "Please."

The shoes had straps with buttons and I had to help. Aunt Gerda eased off Fern's black shoulder purse and set it on the counter top. Then she turned to me. "Matthew? I'm going to have to ask you to wait outside. Fern is very modest."

"Oh . . . well . . . sure!" I could feel my face getting warm. "I'll just wait on the front porch."

The heavy wooden front door had been open all the way. I'd bumped it when I carried Fern in. Now it had swung forward, and when I went to push it back, I saw a piece of paper pinned to it. The paper was ruled and had three holes punched in the margin and a torn border as if it had been ripped out of a notebook. Printed on it in red were the words:

GET OUT OF THE CANYIN AND TAKE YOUR CREEPY GHOST CHILDREN WITH YOU. WE MEAN BUSNESS.

I pulled it off the door and read it again. Two words spelled wrong. Not that that was much of a clue. The world was filled with bad spellers. Mrs. Valdoni was terrible. She told me once she couldn't spell her married name for the first three years. But surely Mr. Terlock wouldn't write a note like this? And a real estate agent or property buyer, whatever, would surely know how to spell "canyon" unless he was faking it.

I was still looking at the note, hoping for a clue that wasn't there, when a voice called out in back of me. I almost jumped out of my skin. Had the vigilantes come back? Or was it one of the dolls . . . the ghost children? My neck hurt as I creaked it around to peer behind.

A girl sat on a too-small bike at the end of the path, balancing with her feet on the ground on either side.

"Who did this to Gerda's kids?" she asked. "I swear, this is the worst." She walked forward, straddling the bike. I couldn't believe the way she did that, holding on to the handlebars, spinning to lay the bike on the ground. Now she was running up the path.

"Oh, George!" she said to a doll who wore weird-looking knickerbocker pants. "Just look at you! And Arabella! The dress Gerda made for you just last week! It's ruined. She must be sick about this." The dolls seemed to listen, smiling their never-ending smiles. "But where's Fern?" she asked then. "What happened to her?"

She glared accusingly at me, hands on hips.

"Fern's inside," I said. "Aunt Gerda's cleaning her up."

"Oh. And you're Matthew, of course. I'm Kristin. It was my dad who brought you and your sister from the bus stop. Slim Ericson. I don't know why he's called 'Slim.' He isn't slim at all."

"Only Aunt Gerda calls me Matthew. I'm really Matt."

She nodded, staring hard at me. I was staring hard at her, too.

"I thought you'd be taller," she said. "Gerda told me you're a year older than I am, but I think I'm definitely bigger."

I stood as big as I could. "No way," I said. But she did have really long legs. That was how she was able to do that neat thing with the bike. Or maybe her legs only looked long because her shorts were so short and because the man's white shirt she wore almost hid them entirely.

"Anyway, hi, Matthew." She ran up the front steps, pulling off the bent-out-of-shape tennis hat she wore, letting her long blond hair tumble down. "What have you got there?" she asked.

I was still holding the note and I gave it to her. "This was on the door."

She read it and handed it back. I hoped she hadn't noticed that she definitely was taller than I was.

"Dorks," she said, drumming her fingers on the porch rail. "I guess all this happened last night."

"Yes. We didn't hear anything."

She turned to push open the door and I said: "Wait a sec. I don't think we should tell Aunt Gerda about the note. Not yet anyway. She's upset enough."

Kristin nodded. "Aren't you coming in?"

"Oh, no. Aunt Gerda wants me to wait outside."

"How come? You mean, in case the dorks come back?"

I shrugged. No way was I going to tell her I wasn't allowed to see a girl doll in her underwear.

I heard Kristin speak to Derek as she went past. "Well, I see you escaped. I suppose you had your turn already with all that paint. That's a sharp-looking jacket Gerda's making for you."

I shook my head. Another one who talked to blocks of wood. She said something to Aunt Gerda then and I heard the high little polite pipe of Abby's voice. They were all talking now, and I recognized a word here and there. "Truck" and "Mom has something . . ." and "cold water." Maybe they'd put a robe on Fern and I'd be able to go back inside. For now, though, I'd have to wait.

I sat in one of the rockers.

The long grass in the front yard moved softly in the breeze, and the dolls moved, too, in a stiff little dance. I tried not to watch them or to think about them either.

High in the sky a hawk hung, circled, flew out of my sight. A bluejay hopped down to the yard, found a plum pit, and took off with it. Abby had left the two plastic bags on the other chair and I got up, rolled them into a ball, and went down the path. The road on either side of Aunt Gerda's lay sun-filled, dusty, empty.

I walked around the side to the back yard. Here was the old shed, tilted as crazily as the house, and beside it the vegetable garden I'd seen from the window. Summer squash lay tangled in the long grass, some as long as blown-up yellow balloons. A clothesline with pins stretched between two trees. And there was the swing. I inspected the ropes before I let myself look at what I knew I'd come round here to see.

The grave wasn't overgrown like the rest of the yard. The grass had been carefully shaved away from the rectangle of earth. Beneath the cross was a vase of flowers, wilted but not yet brown; I remembered the roses Abby and I put on our mother's grave. They'd be dust by now.

The cross had an inscription.

I stepped closer, careful not to put my feet on that neat patch of earth. Burned into the wood were the words:

HERE LIES HARRIETTE, DEARLY BELOVED DAUGHTER OF
JOSEPH AND GERDA YOURRA. REST IN PEACE.

I bit at my knuckles. Harriette? So there'd been eight children, then, and it was the last one who'd died. I walked backward, needing to get away. What did I mean, it was the last one who died? Dolls don't die.

5

"MATT? MATT?" That was Abby calling from the front of the house.

"I'm coming," I yelled, but she was coming, too. I didn't want her to see that grave, though she'd have to, wouldn't she, sooner or later? And I guess nothing is supposed to be as frightening when you face up to it. That's what Mrs. Valdoni had said when I didn't want to go to the mortuary after Mom died.

"We're going to have breakfast," Abby announced, appearing around the corner. "Aunt Gerda says she forgot we hadn't eaten yet and what do we want. She says Kristin can eat with us, too." Abby had put her shoes back on and I bent to tie the laces.

"Good," I said. "Do you want to try the swing for a minute, Ab?"

"Yes! Aunt Gerda says we won't have the tea party today. Not till we get all the dolls looking nice again."

I nodded and held the wooden swing seat so she could climb onto it, pushing to get her started.

"I can do it myself. I can. Don't push anymore," she ordered, so I stood back and let her pump her skinny legs up and down while I thought about how to handle this.

"We'd better go in and get breakfast," I said after a while. "But I want to show you something first."

I took her warm little hand as we walked toward Harriette's grave. It wasn't hard to know exactly when she spotted the cross. Her fingers tightened around mine.

"One of the dolls is buried here," I said in a matter-of-fact way. "I guess something happened. Aunt Gerda probably had a pretty funeral for it, the kind we had at home for your china horse when it broke. Remember?"

Abby stood sucking on the fingers of her other hand.

Just don't remember Mom's funeral, Abby, I thought. Don't remember the wet churchyard, the rain dripping from Mrs. Valdoni's umbrella, the sticky, brown mud. "I bet Aunt Gerda put those flowers there," I said. "Do you remember we brought flowers for the china horse?"

Abby stared up at me with her big, dark eyes. "His name was Snowy, Matt."

"I know. We wrapped up the pieces of china in a tissue and put them in a shoe box."

Abby was nodding now, really into the storytelling.

She looked at the grave. "Is Aunt Gerda's dolly in a box down there?"

"I expect so. Her name was Harriette."

"Did she break?"

"I guess." For the life of me I couldn't think how a wooden doll with no joints could break, but I wasn't going to say that to Abby. She skipped along beside me as we walked back to the house. So the doll's grave hadn't bothered her that much after all. Not as much as it had bothered me.

The plum-pocked family swung gently to watch us as we passed. Abby stopped. "You poor things. If I had the person who did this to you I'd . . . I'd just spit on him. I would. Do you think it was those viggie-lantern people, Matt?"

"I don't know, Ab. I have no idea. But I wish you wouldn't talk to the dolls as if they're people. Would you please quit doing that, Ab?"

"How come you sound so mad?" Abby asked. "You don't get mad when I talk to my teddy."

"That's different. Come on."

In the kitchen, Kristin was scooping yogurt from a cardboard tub into three blue bowls. An opened can of raspberries was on the table and she spooned some of the fruit on top.

"Yumbos," Abby said, smacking her lips and climbing into a chair. Derek beamed from his stand and Fern stood by the sink, her back to us. Aunt Gerda knelt in front of her, her mouth full of pins.

Fern wore a blue dress now, the hem partly pinned up, the rest hanging down to cover her feet. The dress had a white lacy collar and it was too big everywhere. Aunt Gerda had the waist nipped in and there were great pinned folds on the shoulders.

"Is that one of your own dresses, Aunt Gerda?" I asked, but before she could take the pins from her mouth to answer, Abby spoke for her.

"No. Aunt Gerda goes to the dump. She finds thing people have thrown away and washes them and keeps them for the children."

I could tell I was going to have to get mad at her for calling them children, too. But not right now. Right now I was wondering how long the clothes Ab and I had would last. When they wore out, would Aunt Gerda expect *us* to wear dump clothes, too?

Ab pointed with her spoon to a wicker hamper. "Aunt Gerda has a whole *basketful* of stuff. It's amazing the good things people throw away." Her voice was such an exact imitation of Aunt Gerda's that it made Kristin laugh. Abby kills me, too, the way she can mimic grownups.

"Aunt Gerda doesn't find many boy things, though," she went on. "She'll have to make them and it's hard for her because she doesn't see well enough to sew these days. Aunt Gerda's got jewelry, too. A bag full of it."

Fern had spun around to face us now and Abby put down her spoon. "Oooh, she's so pretty in that dress. Was Harriette that pretty?"

My warning glance came too late.

"What happened to poor Harriette?" Abby asked.

"We saw the grave," I said quickly. "We just wondered."

Aunt Gerda took the pins from her mouth and stuck them in a red pincushion she wore like an oversized watch on her wrist.

"Harriette met with an accident. It almost broke our hearts. And yes, Abigail, she was very pretty. Very pretty and very sweet."

In the silence I heard the clink of Kristin's spoon on her bowl. Her hair swung forward hiding her face. What did she think of all this? Did she think it was loony tunes, too?

"My Snowy met with an accident," Abby said. "He fell off the table."

"Snowy was a horse," I explained.

Kristin raised her eyebrows. "And he fell off the table?"

"A china horse," I said.

"What kind of accident was Harriette's?" Abby asked. "Did she fall, too?"

"Ab! Maybe she doesn't want to talk about it," I said.

Aunt Gerda jabbed a pin in and out of the pincushion. "That's all right, Abigail. However, I don't ever discuss it in front of the other children. Harriette *was* their sister, after all."

Abby nodded wisely, looking from Fern to Derek.

"Well, I'm sure you haven't had enough to eat,

Matthew, dear, or you either, Abigail," Aunt Gerda said.

Not to change the subject or anything, I thought.

"There's cereal in the glass case under the counter," she went on, "and milk in the refrigerator. Take whatever you want."

"I like living in a little shop," Abby said as she and I chose a box of Crispie Cornballs from the display case. I wiped the dust from the package on the leg of my jeans. "Do you want some, Kristin?"

Kristin shook her head. "No thanks, I'm full."

As soon as I tasted the cereal, I knew why she'd turned it down. Maybe ten years ago this stuff had been fresh. Abby didn't seem to notice.

By the time we'd finished and washed the bowls, Fern's dress had been pinned all the way around. Her wooden legs and feet were very pale and smooth as silk. Someone had painted her toenails pink. Looking at them gave me the creeps.

Aunt Gerda repinned the plastic butterfly clip that held Fern's hair back from her face. "Maybe the white beads and earrings, Fern, dear. What do you think?"

It seemed to me we were all listening, waiting for Fern's answer, which, thank goodness, didn't come.

"Shall we search through the jewelry bag, Abigail, and see what we can find?"

"Yeah!" Abby clapped her hands.

"And Matthew. I'm sure you don't want to look through a bag of jewelry. So why don't you go out to the shed. There's a bike out there for you."

"A bike?"

"It was your uncle Joseph's. Here!" She took a key from a hook behind the counter and gave it to me.

I turned it around in my hand. "I've never had a bike, Aunt Gerda," I said slowly. "I'll take good care of it. Thanks. Thanks a lot."

"You're welcome, dear. Kristin? Can you show him where the shed is?"

"Can I go, too, Aunt Gerda?" Abby asked. "I want to see Matt's bike. I'll look for Fern's jewelry after."

"Of course, dear."

Ab bounced up and down as we walked to the back. "Maybe I can get a bike, too, Matt. In the dump, maybe."

"Maybe." I unlocked the door.

The inside of the shed was dim and smelled of damp. Dust floated in the pale sunbeams that poked through the two windows. The bike was balanced on its kickstand way in the back. I saw that there was a rusted lawnmower in the shed, too, and a chair with torn canvas and a bunch of tools. On the floor were several thick blocks of wood, and sawdust was every-where. It puffed up around our feet as we walked through it. A dingy bed sheet was draped over some-thing on a workbench.

"Have you been in here before?" I whispered to Kristin.

She shook her head. "This was where your uncle made the children." Kristin was whispering, too, and I knew why. There was something strange in here, a

49

feeling, a too quiet quiet. Silly, I told myself. This was my uncle's workshop, period. A place like my mother's studio with its easel and piles of canvases and tubes of paint.

Abby stood close to the door. "I don't like it in here," she whined. "It's scary."

"It's O.K., Ab. It's O.K."

I lifted the kickstand with my foot and wheeled the bike to the door without looking right or left, edging Kristin and Abby out ahead of me. The air felt good. I took a breath of it and locked the door behind us.

Kristin pointed down at the bike. "You're going to have to pump the tires, Matt."

The bike was an old three-speed with shiny black paint. The handlebars hadn't a speck of rust and the rims and spokes of the wheels had been coated with some kind of preserving grease. I loved it. But Kristin was right. Both tires were perfectly flat.

"All I need is a pump," I said. "Do you have one, Kristin?"

"No. But I saw one in the shed, on the pegboard in the back."

"Oh." There was a bell fastened to the bike's handlebars. I tried it and it worked. *Ching, ching, ching.* I let Abby ring it while I spun the pedals and checked the chain. I pummeled the seat and rubbed the sawdust off it with my elbow. Then I rang the bell again.

"Well," I said at last. "I guess I'd better go get the pump."

"I don't want to go in there again," Abby whispered.

I didn't either. But I wasn't going to let Kristin see what a wimp I was. "Stay here with Kristin, Ab, and hold the bike. I'll be back."

I unlocked the door and grinned back at them. See? See how brave? I may be small, but I'm spunky.

Inside, I walked fast, grabbed the pump off the wall, hurried back past the workbench. Almost in spite of itself my hand reached out, lifted a corner of the stained sheet. Why was I doing this? Just get out, I told myself. Get out. But then my eyes saw the block of wood, the pale, soft wood that was beginning to turn into one of the dolls.

There was the rounded shape of the head, the small curve of the neck, the slope of the shoulders, the waist, the legs, still blocked together. No face, though, and no arms or hands or feet. Sweat cold as ice trickled down inside my shirt as I dropped the sheet and ran for the door.

6

"MATT? ARE YOU O.K.?" Kristin asked.

"Sure, I'm O.K."

I worked the pump a few times to try it, whistling carelessly, then bent to unscrew the cap from the front-tire valve. What had I seen in there? Just a piece of wood, a doll Uncle Joseph must have started before he died, three years ago. Don't get carried away, Matt!

My hand was shaking so much I had trouble screwing pump and tire together, but I did and began filling the tire with air. When it was filled, I started to work on the back one. Abby had to have a turn, too, of course, puffing and panting and gritting her teeth.

I patted her on the shoulder. "You did great, Ab."

Kristin flashed me the nicest smile.

I tried the bike then, riding round the side of the house and up the path to the porch where Aunt Gerda stood, leaning on the railing.

"How is it?" she asked.

I gave her the thumbs-up sign, then rang the bell. "Perfect. I can't believe it's mine. I asked for a bike three Christmases in a row, but Mom couldn't handle it, and I was saving, too, but . . ."

I rang the bell again instead of finishing. No point in going into the way our money had disappeared after Mom's medications started. "It's a terrific bike," I added. "They don't build them like this anymore." I wasn't sure about that, but I'd heard people say that about old cars and I thought it would please Aunt Gerda. It did.

She watched while I wheeled Abby down the path, Ab ringing the bell so fiercely that a bunch of blackbirds screeched up from the trees. The dolls watched, too. Then Kristin tried the bike. I was happy to see that her feet didn't touch the ground when she rode, especially since I was having trouble even reaching the pedals. Maybe I could lower the seat a bit.

"Abigail?" Aunt Gerda said. "I've poured all the jewelry on the table. Do you want to come in now and help Fern decide?"

"Yeah!" Abby gamboled up the path.

How was I *ever* going to get her to stop thinking of the dolls as people when Aunt Gerda talked about them this way? As if Fern had any say in which jewelry they put on her!

I looked at my aunt waiting for Ab on the porch and I was filled with all kinds of mixed-up feelings. There was gratitude. What would we have done without her? Her letters had cheered Mom up. The little bits and pieces of money she'd sent had helped with the groceries and the rent, and I could see now that she probably had to sacrifice to send it because this shop wasn't exactly a gold mine.

I remembered the way she'd said "Come" when Mom died, how loving she'd been with us last night. But I knew I was scared of her, too, the way you are when you sense someone isn't like everyone else. When you sense the someone is different. I wished Blinky was here so I could talk this over with him. Blinky was always real easy to talk to. Maybe I should call him? Or Mrs. Valdoni? But I'd have to find a phone someplace, and anyway, what could I say? How could I explain this?

Aunt Gerda put her arm around Ab so they could go in the house together, but Ab turned, stiffened her little legs and called back to me: "Don't go off somewhere without me, Matt. Promise?"

"Promise," I said.

"I'll cry if you go," she said.

"I won't, Ab. I'll be just out here in front, where you can see me if you come on the porch."

She nodded. "O.K."

"You're really nice to her, you know it?" Kristin said.

I shrugged. "Abby's O.K."

"I'm not that nice to Fee."

"Fee?"

"My little brother, Frank Edmund Ericson."

"Fee's probably got both a mom and a dad," I said.

"Yes." Kristin gave me a strange, soft kind of look, then pulled her white hat from the pocket of her shorts and jammed it back on her head. She picked up her bike and straddled it. I thought it was so cool the way she did that, like a cowboy on a horse.

We rode up the road a bit and back. Part of the time I could see the roof of the shed where the doll lay on its carving board. I could see the sun gleaming black on the side windows and I imagined how hot it would be in there now, and the smell of the sawdust. It would be even hotter under the sheet. Quit it, Matt! Turn it off!

Cars passed us, heading into the canyon. I noticed how they slowed at Aunt Gerda's to stare at the dolls. They'd be wondering what they were or, if they'd seen them before, what had happened to them. Some of the people were probably admiring them, others would be annoyed like Mr. Terlock and think they ruined the beauty of the canyon. A few of the drivers waved to us as they went by. One guy rolled down his window. "Hey, Kristin," he yelled. "How come you're not operating your stall today?"

"I'm taking a vacation," Kristin said.

"Too bad." The guy grinned. "I was planning on buying."

"I might open later," Kristin said. "Catch you on your way out."

"What do you sell in your stall?" I asked when he'd whizzed past in a cloud of dust. "Lemonade?"

Kristin rolled her eyes. "Give me a break! No, not lemonade." But she didn't tell me what.

"Lots of cars," I said when a couple more had passed.

"It's Saturday. On Saturdays and Sundays people pour in here. They hike and picnic and look at the art and stuff. The canyon's full of artists and they put out their paintings every weekend. Dealers come all the time."

I stared at her. "Real dealers? Important ones?"

"I guess. They come up from L.A."

I rode ahead of her, made a wide arc and came back. Real dealers! Imagine if I put out Mom's art and one came and saw the canvases. Imagine if he said: "These are incredible. A new, wonderful talent." I'd ask Aunt Gerda if I could set up a table, or maybe she had a workbench . . . my mind flicked to the work-bench in the shed. Not that one.

Abby came to the porch, saw me, and waved.

"She's checking," Kristin said softly and I nodded.

We'd stopped in front of the house. It was getting hotter by the minute now and I peeled off my T-shirt and tied it around my waist.

"I have to go," Kristin said. "Duty calls."

Would she let me share her stall if I asked? Maybe I could bring over some of Mom's paintings and then, when people stopped for whatever they bought from her, they'd see them. Did I dare suggest it? Now? And there were a bunch of other things I wanted to know, too, if she'd tell me.

"I was going to ask you something," I said.

"Yeah? What?"

I ran my hands over the greasy handlebars of the bike. Maybe it was too soon to bring up about the paintings. I'd show them to her first, explain about Mom. "Well . . ."

I stared beyond her to the dolls standing still as statues on the grass. Should I ask what happened to Harriette? Or if she'd ever heard the dolls talk? Or . . .

Another car drove by with a screech of its horn.

"I have to go," Kristin said impatiently. "I'm losing customers by the minute."

"Do you know this guy Terlock?" I blurted out.

"Gene Terlock? Sure. He lives farther back in the canyon. He's got no kids, but I think he and his wife are pretty rich. They own a bunch of houses. He's one of the crowd who wants to get rid of Gerda."

"I know. He was here this morning. With his vigilantes."

Kristin made a face. "He was here again?"

"Do you think he could be the one who messed up the dolls?"

Kristin stared hard at me and then slowly shook her head. "I doubt it. It's not . . . not businesslike enough. I think Gene Terlock would always do things properly, you know. He'd come out with some kind of papers and tell Aunt Gerda she had to leave by sundown."

I nodded. "Of course, maybe he did it this way so nobody would suspect him."

"Maybe."

"Well, how about Clay Greeley?" I asked. "Do you know him?"

"I sure do. The Greeleys live down the road. There's just Clay and his dad. How do *you* know him?"

I told her about the three guys last night and I propped up the bike and sprinted to the porch for the two white plastic bags. "These stink of plums," I said.

Kristin took the bags, looked inside, sniffed at them.

"Of course, someone else could have done it," I said. "One of the vigilantes or . . ."

Kristin interrupted. "Somebody *could*, but I bet Clay and those two geek friends of his *did*. That's just like Clay Greeley. I swear, he's such a bully. One time he got hold of Fee and he pushed his head down and made the poor little guy eat grass before he'd let him up."

"Why?"

"Just 'cause Clay Greeley thought it was funny. I got him in school, though. I punched him out good." Kristin scratched at a mosquito bite on her leg.

"You punched out a boy?"

"Sure. I'd punch out a boy any time I felt like it. That Clay's slime time. Little kids, old ladies . . . want to go get him?"

"Now?" I asked.

"Sure now."

"I'd have to take Ab."

"You could tell her we have to go someplace and we'll be back in a half an hour."

"No. And anyway, I'd want to take her. I wouldn't leave her here with . . ." I stopped.

"Are you afraid of the dolls, or Gerda?" Kristin's voice was cold as stone.

"Well, I'm not afraid, exactly. It's just . . ."

Kristin glared at me. "Great. You're just like everyone else. You think Gerda's bonkers and you're scared she might hurt Abby or something. That's it, isn't it?" A bee bigger than any I'd ever seen came buzzing around our heads. I swiped at it and it took off.

"I know she wouldn't hurt Ab," I said. "But she does act kind of funny."

"Wouldn't you if you were here all alone with only a bunch of dolls to talk to? If hardly anybody ever came in your shop anymore, and you had no money, and nobody to turn to, and the phone company took out your phone, and you can't pay the electric bill, and you think one of these days you're going to lose your home and you'll have to go live in an old people's home?"

"Listen," I said feebly, trying to hide my embarrassment. Were things *that* bad for Aunt Gerda? And still she'd sent for us?

"No, you listen. Gerda's just the sweetest, kindest person in the whole world. She came to our house every day, every single day, when Mom caught chickenpox from Fee or me, and we were all sick. My mom's left Fee with her a bunch of times. Do you

59

think my mom would leave Fee with a crazy lady? You have some nerve, Matt O'Meara."

I was getting pretty mad myself. "Why don't you just cool it," I said. "My mom left me in charge of Ab. I look out for her, that's all."

We were glaring at each other now and I wished I'd let her go when she'd wanted to. I'd never ask to share her stall. I'd set up one of my own. "I thought you had to go," I said pointedly.

A big, fancy station wagon with wood trim pulled up outside the house.

"It's Mr. Stengel," Kristin muttered. "He's a friend of Gerda's."

"Oh. My mistake. I thought you said she didn't *have* any friends," I said in a rotten, sneering way I can pull out if I try.

It was wasted on Kristin. She was walk-straddling the bike down the path, calling "Hi, Mr. Stengel" to the man who was getting out of the car.

He wore a white suit and a pink shirt and he was the smallest, most perfect little old man I'd ever seen. I tried not to stare, but it was hard. This guy wasn't much bigger than I am.

Kristin dropped her bike at the end of the path and I followed and propped mine beside it. I was still holding the bags and I jammed them into my jeans pocket.

"Hello, Kristin." The man's gaze went past her to the dolls. "What on earth . . . ?" His voice was strange, too, high and squeaky.

"It happened last night. Some slime did it."

Mr. Stengel took out a pink handkerchief and wiped the top of his head, which was bald and perspiring. "This is terrible. How is poor Mrs. Yourra?"

"She's upset. But she'll be O.K. This is Matt. He and his sister are living here now."

Mr. Stengel had a warm smile that crinkled his eyes and made furrows on his smooth forehead. "Hello, Matt. Mrs. Yourra told me you were coming. She was looking forward to it. What a shame someone had to do this!" He tut-tutted, looking at the dolls, then held out his hand for me to shake. "It looks like they're starting to harass your aunt again," he said. "Sometimes I think her life would be easier if she got rid of the dolls."

"She never will, Mr. Stengel," Kristin said. "You know that."

"I know. It's too bad people have to be so cruel."

Kristin looked directly at me. "They can be cruel all right."

Aunt Gerda and Abby had come out on the porch and Mr. Stengel went up and spoke softly to Aunt Gerda and shook hands in a grown-up way with Abby. Even from here I could see Ab was overcome.

We all sat on the porch, Aunt Gerda and Mr. Stengel in the rockers, the three of us on the steps.

Aunt Gerda brought out lemonade.

"Have you told the police what happened, Mrs. Yourra?" Mr. Stengel asked.

"I see no point in it. The Sierra Maria police

haven't been too sympathetic to me or the children. They have had complaints, of course, and then there was that petition Gene Terlock produced to have me remove the children from the front yard. The police didn't seem to understand when I told them the children like it out here where they can see the traffic passing."

We sat silently, watching the cars and campers cruise by. Aunt Gerda sighed: "I wish people wouldn't take it out on the children, though. I can handle anything: words scrawled on the wall, letters. But the children are so innocent."

There was another silence as we looked at them, standing in their innocence. I wormed my hand under the bags in my right-hand pocket and touched the hate-filled note. There'd been others like this, then. This one wasn't the first.

"Ah, well." Aunt Gerda smiled shakily at Mr. Stengel. "Are you out on an art hunt today, Mr. Stengel?"

"Indeed. I've heard that a very good young artist has just moved into a cottage on Tor Point." He glanced at his watch. "In fact, I have an appointment for a showing. I should be on my way." He drained the rest of his lemonade and set the glass down on the wicker table.

I thumped mine down on the porch steps. "You . . . ah . . . buy art?" Something strange seemed to have happened to my breathing.

"That's right." Mr. Stengel smiled his crinkly smile.

"Are you interested in purchasing some, young man?" He stood and whipped a card from the pocket of his jacket.

HAROLD STENGEL: BLACK ORCHID GALLERY
3424 LA CIENEGA BLVD., LOS ANGELES

"Actually," I said, "my mom is an artist. She was. She died."

"Do you remember the painting in my living room, Mr. Stengel?" Aunt Gerda asked quickly. "The one of the beach and the house on the cliff?"

"Indeed. Certainly." There was something in the smooth way he answered that made me think he didn't remember it at all and was just being polite.

"I could show it to you again," I said. "And we have others."

"I would definitely be interested, Matthew, but not today. I'm overloaded with appointments." He helped Aunt Gerda up. "Now, Mrs. Yourra, do you have any of those wonderful cans of clams left? I can't find them anywhere but in your shop. And I could use some more of that Tate and Lyle syrup for my morning pancakes and that English jelly." He took Aunt Gerda's arm and they went in the house, she so big and Mr. Stengel so small. I decided that must be pretty much the way Kristin and I would look if we stood together.

"You know what?" Kristin whispered. "I think Mr. Stengel comes because he likes Gerda . . . you know, *likes* her. I just figured that out. Wouldn't it be great if he wanted to marry her? Wouldn't it be super? He's rich, *plus* he's nice."

"But they're so old," I said. "Both of them."

"So?" Kristin was glaring at me. "What about it?"

For a minute there she seemed to have gotten over being mad at me. Now I could see she was getting ready to begin again.

"Nothing about it," I said quickly. "It would be great."

I went slowly inside, watching as Mr. Stengel made his choices and Aunt Gerda put them in a brown paper sack. Did I dare? Did I? She was making change out of a black purse when I ran up the stairs and grabbed the portfolio.

"Wait till he sees these!" I told Mom's portrait. "He's talking about a new young artist! Just wait till he sees your pictures." I came out so fast I skidded on the rug.

Downstairs, the screen door slammed and Aunt Gerda called: "Matthew? Mr. Stengel is leaving now."

"Too late," I told Mom. "But don't worry. Next time I'll be quicker."

We stood at the bottom of the path, waving as he left, and I called "Come back soon" louder than anyone.

"I've got to take off, too," Kristin said and I went with her to her bike.

"I'm sorry I got mad at you," she said. "It's just

Gerda has it so rough, and you were so nerdy about her."

"I was not."

"O.K., O.K. Anyway, do you want to go tomorrow and tackle that creep Greeley?"

"I don't know if I can," I said. "I mean, Abby . . ."

"Oh, sure. Abby."

I glanced at Kristin suspiciously. Did she think I was only using Ab as an excuse? I couldn't tell what she was thinking as she gazed up at the sky where the hawk was somersaulting again.

"I'm not afraid of Greeley, if that's what you're trying to say," I told her. "Anyway, we're not sure if he's the one who did it."

Kristin shrugged. "Well, I'm going. You can come if you want."

"Why are *you* going? She's not *your* aunt."

"She's my friend. That's just as good. And I've known her a lot longer than you have."

"Well, I'm going, too, then. I'll fix it somehow with Ab."

"Fine. Do you want to come to church with us?"

"Church?" I paused. "I don't know. Does Aunt Gerda go?"

"We used to pick her up every Sunday but not anymore. She won't leave her children."

"Oh. Well, I'll have to see. I'll skip it for tomorrow, though. Thanks anyway."

"I'll come by after lunch, then." She turned from

me and walked toward the dolls. "Bye, kids. See you tomorrow."

I waited, half expecting to hear a chorus of "Byes," knowing how crazy it was but expecting it anyway. But the only sound was a high distant shriek and I saw that the hawk had swooped and was streaking up into the sky carrying something small and furry in his talons.

7

THAT NIGHT I asked Aunt Gerda where I should keep the bike. I had no lock and there was no way I was going to leave it outside, where anyone could steal it. "Should I bring it in the house?" I asked, hoping, and hoping she wouldn't say: "Put it in the shed, Matthew. That door has a lock."

"It will be perfectly safe on the porch," she said instead. "I plan on being out there all night."

"All night? Till morning?" I asked, sounding stupid and probably looking stupid, too. Mrs. Valdoni and I had sat up all night with Mom three times, but that was different.

Aunt Gerda was opening a can of Dinty Moore beef stew, emptying it into a pot on the stove. "I won't leave the children unprotected again."

"But . . ." Didn't she know she couldn't sit up with them every night? She'd have to sleep sometime.

It was as if she knew what I was thinking because

she smiled. "Don't worry, Matthew. You don't need as much rest when you get older. And I'll be quite comfortable. I may doze off, but I'll be visible anyway, right there under the porch light."

That was one of the things that was worrying me. Would she be safe? What was to stop someone from skulking out there in the darkness and throwing plums at her? Or from doing something worse?

"Why don't we just bring the dolls inside," I said. "That would be easier." I gave a fake smile. "They'd be company for Derek and Arabella." Derek smiled at me from his stand by the couch. Aunt Gerda and Abby had worked all day on Fern's dress and now she was outside again and Arabella stood in her place.

Arabella was pinned into a flowered sundress that left her wooden shoulders and arms bare, and Abby was busily trying hats on her, standing on a stool to reach, standing back to get the effect. I'd almost protested when she got a hand mirror so Arabella could see herself, but what was the use? I decided I'd wait till we were alone to remind Ab again that this was only play.

Aunt Gerda stirred the stew with a wooden spoon. "I have considered bringing the children in," she said. "But that would be like submitting to these people. What right have they to tell me what to do on my own property? Why should the children have to move?"

"But I'm worried about you being out there." I lowered my voice so Abby wouldn't hear. "Look, why don't I sleep outside, too. Just in case." The thought of the night, the dolls moving restlessly in the dark, made me shiver, but that was silly. They'd be no more frightening in the night than in the day.

Aunt Gerda touched my hand. "No, Matthew. A boy needs his sleep and I'll be perfectly fine. But thank you. Now . . ." She lifted the pot from the stove and spooned stew into three blue bowls, steam rising, wafting in my direction.

"It smells great," I said.

"Yes. We won't go hungry. There's enough food in the shop to do us for a long time."

Since hardly anyone's buying, I thought, except maybe Mr. Stengel and a few old friends. Still, it was a relief to know there was lots to eat.

She pointed to the zucchini and onion salad on the table. "And we always have the garden."

"*I'd* like to learn how to garden," I said.

"See?" She gave me another smile. "They can't get us down."

Later that night she came in our room to hear my little sister's prayers and to tuck us in. Then I read *Goodnight Moon* twice to Ab, watching and waiting for her eyes to close, which they usually do by the time we get to "Goodnight mittens." Tonight, too.

I lay very still then, listening. Was Aunt Gerda outside already? No, because I could hear her talking softly to someone in her bedroom across the hall. Was it one of the dolls? Nervousness twitched inside me and it was hard not to be scared, hard not to listen for a change of voice if a doll should answer. I tiptoed across to our door and opened it.

The house was so old that nothing fitted properly, and I could see the light gleaming through the crack underneath and through the space at the side of Aunt Gerda's door. I could hear through that space, too, when I got closer.

"I wish you were here to share things with me, Joseph. Nothing was ever as hard when you were with me, not even Harriette's death. I'm strong, though. I'm strong enough to handle this. But now it's not only myself and the children. I have Matthew and little Abby. They're dear to me already, as dear as their mother was to us. This is the only home they have now, Joseph. I won't let anyone force us out of it."

There was a squeaking sound, as if she'd risen from a chair with sagging springs, and then her footsteps coming quickly in my direction.

I stood, numbed. No time to dash back across the hall. She'd find me for sure. I pressed myself against the wall where I'd be behind the door when she opened it. I heard her come out. If she closed the door now, there I'd be. What would she think of me, spying on her like this? What did I think of myself? Not much.

She left the door open. Through a gap by the hinges I saw her walk along the hall. She was carrying a gray blanket, and round her shoulders was the kind of navy pea coat that sailors wear in Seattle. I flattened myself against the cold plaster and held my breath till she disappeared down the stairs. Then I slid out of my hiding place. It wasn't that I'd meant to listen, I told myself. I'd just wondered who she was talking to, and now I knew. It wasn't to one of the dolls; it was to her dead husband. Was that any better?

But then I glanced into her room and saw the photograph on her wall. The man with the stiff collar and the mustache that did nothing to hide his gentle smile would be Uncle Joseph. She'd been talking to his picture the way I do to Mom's. I'd never thought I was crazy, had I? Great the way I'd decided *she* was.

All in all I didn't feel real good about myself as I got my little alarm clock, set it by the light from the landing, and got back into my cot.

Even though we'd left the curtains open and some light from the landing came round and under the door, the room was pretty dark. I thought about the tool shed below. The half-finished doll was probably a girl since they would have wanted a girl to replace Harriette. Her name would start with and "I," since "I" came after "H." Isabel? Iris?

I punched up my pillow, molded it around my head, and tried to make myself think about nice things, like Mr. Stengel's beaming at me: "These are your mother's paintings? They're wonderful. She was truly a magnificent artist."

But I couldn't get the thinking to work and I turned over and drifted into sleep.

It was the alarm that woke me at 3 A.M. I stifled it on the second ring, before it could waken Ab. 3 A.M.! The time I'd set it for. I got up, pulled on my jeans and sweatshirt, and went quietly out of the room. The house was filled with light. What was it Kristin had said about the electric bill? There'd be a big one this month, all right.

When I stood at the top of the stairs, I could see Derek and Arabella. Aunt Gerda must have moved them so they could stand together, because they sure as heck hadn't moved themselves.

Derek's jacket and T-shirt were off and his chunky polished chest and stomach were bare. His skin gleamed as if it had been polished. Maybe he'd smell of lemon, like Mrs. Valdoni's furniture.

Arabella had added white lacy gloves to her outfit and there was a sparkly pin on the front of her sundress. I couldn't decide if Aunt Gerda's dolls were creepier dressed or undressed. The two of them smiled their welcomes at me as I came down the stairs and I scared myself because I almost said "Hi" to them.

Through the screen door, I saw the lighted porch and the spotlight at the bottom of the front yard that shone toward me like a great, white eye. Crickets chirped in a noisy chorus and from somewhere close came the hollow hoot-hoot of a night owl.

As soon as I pushed open the door, Aunt Gerda rose from her chair and the pea coat slipped from her shoulders. "Matthew? What's the matter? Are you sick?"

I shook my head.

"Abigail?"

"We're fine." I couldn't see the dolls on the grass but I sensed their sightless eyes watching me. Shivers ran up and down my skin. "It's my turn for guard duty," I said. "You go in now and get some sleep."

"Oh, Matthew!" She'd been working on Derek's jacket and she stuck the needle in the lapel and put the pile of fabric on top of her sewing box on the table. "Come here, Matthew!"

The door banged behind me as I went closer and let her take my hands. "My dear, this is the sweetest thing. You actually wakened yourself and came down here . . ." Her eyes brimmed with tears.

"It's O.K.," I said, embarrassed suddenly. "You go get some sleep now. I don't mind."

"I'll do no such thing. But I was going to make myself a cup of hot chocolate. Would you like some? I'd be glad of your company."

"Sure. That sounds great."

We made it together, carried it back to the porch, and sat quietly in the rockers drinking it. I told myself there was a little night breeze now and that was what I was hearing, moving nervously in the trees. It wasn't the dolls whispering. It wasn't. I made myself take a sip of hot chocolate and then sit back. "I was wondering," I said. "Why don't you get a dog, Aunt Gerda?"

"We've had dogs. Our last one was Laird. When he was twelve years old, he was hit by a car, right there in front of the house. Poor old Laird! There's so much traffic in the canyon." She shook her head. "I'd never risk another dog, not unless the yard was fenced, and for now that's out of the question."

"I could build us a fence."

She smiled. "I could help."

There was no traffic in the canyon now, nothing but the monotonous cry of the owl, the crick-crick of the crickets, the night pressing itself against the light around us.

"We had a dog called Jim when your mother was a little girl and stayed here with us in the summers. Every day, when she'd take her sketch pad and go up in the canyon, Jim went, too. He lay behind the door for weeks after she went home. I guess that dog missed her just as much as we did."

The rockers bumped gently on the wooden porch as we moved back and forth. I thumbed away a tear that had started a slow trickle down my cheek. Aunt Gerda packed up Derek's jacket and stood. "I have to try this on him. You just sit there quietly with your memories, dear Matthew. I'll be back in a minute."

I found a tissue in the pocket of my jeans and blew my nose. How long did it take Jim to come out from behind the door? How long did it take him to understand Mom wasn't coming back? Weeks? Months? I know, Jim. I know. I blew my nose again and rocked to ease the pain.

Inside I could hear the murmur of Aunt Gerda's voice as she talked to Derek.

Criminy! I'd forgotten that I was out here in the

dark, alone with the dolls. I sat up stiff and straight and peered into the darkness.

Aunt Gerda pushed open the door. "It's going to fit beautifully, thank goodness." She lowered her voice. "Derek can be difficult."

I nodded. In a strange way I was beginning to understand why she talked to the dolls and treated them as if they were real. It was so lonely here, so silent and still. And it must be extra hard for her, being alone all the time since Uncle Joseph died. Was Kristin right that Mr. Stengel "liked" her?

"I was thinking," I said hesitantly. "Mr. Stengel is very nice."

"Yes." She searched in the box for a thimble.

"Do you know when he'll be back?"

"He's been coming more often now that he has this . . . this new interest." I thought I saw the flicker of a smile in her eyes. "Now he comes about every two weeks. I guess he's hoping I'll change my mind."

So Kristin *was* right after all. But Aunt Gerda wasn't jumping into anything.

"I don't think he remembered Mom's painting," I said.

"I imagine he's seen a lot of paintings. It's probably hard to remember every single one. We'll make sure he sees all of them next time and we'll make sure he remembers."

"That's what I was thinking." We smiled at each other.

I watched her take the pins from the lapel of the

jacket and begin to sew with small, fine strokes. Sleep was beginning to fill my eyes, making it hard for me to keep them open. A yawn swelled like an explosion in my throat. I tried to hide it, but Aunt Gerda saw and laughed. "Go, dear Matthew. Go on to bed. And thank you."

"If you're sure. If there's nothing I can do."

"I'm sure."

I got up and leaned over to hug her. She smelled of chocolate. "Well, anyhow, you're not alone anymore," I said. "You've got me now . . . and Ab."

She patted my cheek. "That's right. And we'll take care of each other. Goodnight, Matthew."

"Goodnight."

I opened the screen door and almost fell over Derek. He was standing just inside, as if watching us, or listening.

"What . . ." I stepped back, the door bumping and slapping itself against my face. Derek grinned at me through the mesh.

"Aunt Gerda," I stuttered. "Derek . . ."

"Oh, I should have warned you. Is he in the way?"

I heard the rustle as she stood up, but I didn't turn. I didn't want to turn my back on Derek.

"Oh." But when had she moved him? When she'd gone inside, while I'd been sitting on the porch. Of course. But I hadn't heard anything. I hadn't even heard the roll of the spool across the floor. Maybe I'd been too deep in my thoughts. Of course, that was what it was.

"Well, goodnight again," I said, edging around Derek, careful not to brush against his smooth, wooden chest. But how silly I'd been to panic like that. I could just see the way Kristin would raise her eyebrows if she knew. Well, she wouldn't know.

Even so, as I went up the stairs, I kept checking back over my shoulder. Just in case Derek was coming after me.

8

KRISTIN HAD said she'd be here at two so we could ride over to Clay Greeley's. We were going to warn him. If he was the one messing with Aunt Gerda and the dolls, he'd better lay off. But Kristin came earlier with her parents and Fee. I was on the porch, polishing my bike, keeping busy so I wouldn't get too nervous about going to Greeley's, when her dad sounded the horn.

Aunt Gerda and Ab came out right away and Kristin introduced us all. Then her mom told Aunt Gerda how sorry she'd been to hear about the children. She meant the dolls, of course, not Ab and me. I was getting used to the children not being us. She and Kristin walked over to admire Derek's new outfit and Arabella's sundress, and Mrs. Ericson said Mr. Ericson had a nice pair of gray pants that were too small for him since he'd put on weight, and she thought they could be altered to fit George, and she'd bring them over.

Mr. Ericson said he'd fit into the pants as soon as his diet started working again and Mrs. Ericson poked his stomach and asked, "What diet?" The way they talked to each other was so friendly and loving it made my throat ache. Had Mom and Dad talked to each other like this? It hurt that I couldn't remember.

The grownups went inside then and Kristin and Fee and Ab and I sat on the porch steps.

"I've got a tortoise," Fee told Abby. "His name's Giant. I painted my phone number on his shell, so if he gets lost he'll know where he lives."

Abby sat up. "I know *my* phone number. It's five five five, four nine three two."

"That's not our number anymore, Ab," I said gently. "That was at home. We don't have a phone here."

"Oh." Ab stuck two fingers in her mouth and Fee said, "You can share mine if you like." He told her his number and the two of them began rhyming it off, giggling and making faces.

"Are we going to Greeley's early?" I asked Kristin. "I thought you said two."

"I did. It's just, we have to stop here some Sundays on the way home from church so Mom and Dad can buy a bunch of groceries from Gerda."

"They *do?*"

"Yeah. She doesn't have much, of course. But Mom says every little bit helps her. She's too proud to take money for nothing. I think my dad has tried."

I nodded. "Your parents are nice. You're lucky."

"I know. Anyway, I'll be back for you around two."

"O.K."

Two was hours away, and I was jumpy already!

She was back at ten after. Ab and I were waiting for her at the end of the path.

"Abby wanted to come," I explained to Kristin, who raised her eyebrows. She didn't have to say "Oh, really?" Her eyebrows said it for her. I didn't say: "She doesn't like me to leave her. I can't help it." I hoped my spread-out hands said that for me.

"Well, anyway, let's go. Clay Greeley will be out at his stall. At least we'll have no trouble finding him." Kristin took off, riding like fury down the road, and I took off after her, standing to pump the pedals, Abby in the bike seat behind me, clutching handfuls of my shirt.

"Hold tight, Ab," I ordered, and I knew I was glad to have her with me even if I wasn't exactly sure why. Maybe I don't like to be separated from her either.

Kristin had said it wasn't far to the Greeley house, but it seemed far, riding in the loose dirt at the edge of the road to stay clear of the traffic. It was hot, even in the shade of the hedges, and Abby's little hands were sweaty through my shirt. My legs felt weak. How humiliating if I had to stop and rest while Kristin raced ahead! She'd think I was slowing because I was scared. Well, I was scared. Scared enough to want to turn tail and jet out of here. I wished Blinky and John were with me. I'd even settle for Knock Knock. The four of us had stood up to the Rawlins gang on the playground that time. Well, Blinky and John and

80

Knock Knock weren't with me now. It was just me and Kristin. I made myself put on a spurt of speed and lessen the gap between us.

And then we swung round a bend in the road and I saw Kristin come to her special brake stop with both feet dragging in the dirt. We were there.

The Greeley house sat in the middle of a bald brown yard, small and poor and neglected. Not newly poor the way Aunt Gerda's was. This one had been that way since the beginning, more like a shelter for animals than a house for people. Part of the roof had caved in and the wooden wall had patches of peeling paint, crusty as scabs.

The best-looking thing around was the stall that had been set up inside the front yard, parallel to the road. I saw it and thought, That's the kind I'll have when I start to sell Mom's paintings. If Mr. Stengel doesn't want them all first. Mine will be sturdy and strong like this, the three clean planks held up by nice sawhorses on either end.

There were two customers in front of the stall and three guys behind it, selling. It wasn't hard to figure them for Clay Greeley and the heavenly twins. I stopped and held the bike while Ab stepped onto the pedals and then to the ground.

"Oh, look Matt!" She was gone, running from me to a cardboard box with a hand-lettered sign: RABBITS FOR SALE. $2. Someone had done a drawing of a rabbit with long floppy ears on the side of the box.

By now the two customers were walking back to

their car and Clay Greeley had spotted us. He said something to one of the twins and the three of them began tittering and staring in our direction.

"Hi, Kristin," Greeley called. "Who are your friends?"

"Don't worry about it. This isn't a friendly visit," Kristin said.

"Let me do this," I whispered.

"Did you think I was coming to just stand around and be quiet?" she whispered back. "Think again."

Now I was getting a good look at Clay Greeley and I was deciding that he wasn't that scary after all. I don't know what I'd been expecting. A monster maybe, straight out of an old Maurice Sendak book, or a dude in a black leather jacket with a switchblade behind his ear.

This guy had a face that was round as a pumpkin and covered with freckles, and his hair was pumpkin colored, too, soft and short and feathery. I sighed with relief. Clay Greeley wasn't even that big. The twins had long pale faces and pale eyes. Mrs. Valdoni would have said they looked sickly, and if they'd lived in our building she'd have told their mother to give them cod liver oil. Cod liver oil was Mrs. Valdoni's answer to everything.

I stopped to look in the rabbit box, which had an old piece of heavy screening laid across the top. "Isn't he darling, Matt?" Abby breathed.

"Go ahead, pick him up, kid. Make yourself at home." Clay Greeley called. "It pays to let customers check out the merchandise. That's what a wise man once told me."

He waved to Kristin and me, inviting us closer. "What can I do for you two?"

Kristin had edged herself ahead of me somehow and I stepped beside her so the two of us were in front of the stall, facing the other three in back.

"If you're the one who's bugging Mrs. Yourra, you can stay away," I said. "I'm Matt O'Meara and I've come to live with her. Me and my sister." I jerked my head in the direction of Ab, who was sitting beside the box now, the rabbit in her lap. Little as Ab is, she'd managed to lift the screening off. I lowered my voice. "If you guys have plans to hassle my aunt anymore, just forget it. I'm here now."

"Oh, wow!" One of the twins nudged the other with his elbow. "Oh, wow, this guy is maxi tough. We have to look out for *this* guy."

"That's right," I said.

There was a wooden crate filled with avocados on the stall in front of me. The sign said AVOCADOES, FOUR FOR A DOLLAR. I wondered if avocados was spelled right because if it wasn't, that might be a clue, but I couldn't tell because I didn't know how to spell it myself. There were some small, bumpy-looking colored rocks marked CRYSTALS, DIFFERENT PRICES, and there were lemons, 10 CENTS EACH, and oranges tied in plastic sacks, the kind I'd found in Aunt Gerda's yard.

"Any *plums* for sale?"

"Plums? Plums?" Clay Greeley grinned at Castor or maybe Pollux. "Do we have any plums?"

"Not anymore." The twin grinned back.

"What he means is, we had plums," Greeley said. "We got trees in back. But we used them up. And what's left are all rotted out."

"Or the birds got them," the other twin said, his pale eyes wide and innocent.

"'Course, sometimes we clean up what's lying on the ground," his brother said. "We like to keep Clay's place neat and tidy."

Kristin jabbed a finger toward Clay Greeley. "We don't want any rotten plums or anything else at Gerda's," she said. "You're such a smut, Greeley. You give me a big, fat pain."

"Aw. He's real worried about that," Castor or Pollux said.

"Yeah." Greeley's grin spread. "I won't be able to sleep tonight I'll be so worried."

"*I* won't be sleeping tonight," I said. "You come near Aunt Gerda's and I'm going to get you. I mean it. Leave her alone."

Greeley and I were almost eyeball to eyeball now, with both of us leaning across the stall, and suddenly I realized that he *was* scary. You just didn't notice it at first. The scary things were his eyes. They didn't go with the round, freckled face and the big, gummy grin. His eyes were adult eyes, the kind of adult who doesn't like anything or anybody. Tough, mean, cold. My heart started hammering.

"So what if we want to get rid of your crazy old aunt," Greeley said. "You can't stop us. We do what we like. And if you want to help her, you'll tell her to get out of our canyon."

"And take her ghost children with her?" I asked. So they *were* the ones. "Write her another letter, why don't you?"

"This bozo's real brave," one twin told the other.

"Well, he'd have to be, wouldn't he, living up there with the witch and the talking dolls."

I glanced nervously over my shoulder at Ab, but she was playing with the rabbit, totally absorbed.

Kristin took over. "She's not a witch and the dolls don't talk. That's the dumbest . . ."

"Yeah?" Clay Greeley's cold eyes stared into mine. "Don't tell that to the twins. They *heard* them."

"Oh, sure," Kristin said sarcastically.

"We heard them all right. And we weren't the only ones. Billy Jackson was with us and Card Killander."

"Sure," Kristin said again. "Great bunch there. And what were the dolls saying, Pollux?"

"He's Pollux." Castor thumbed toward the other twin.

"Go ahead and tell them what you heard," Clay Greeley ordered.

"You want me to?"

"That's what I'm telling you, isn't it?" Clay said impatiently.

"Well, it was real dark. It was about one in the morning and we were just walking past, on the road . . ."

"One in the morning and you were just walking past on the road?" I raised my eyebrows the way Kristin does and tried to sound disbelieving, because I knew I didn't want to hear this and didn't want to believe it if I did hear it. I didn't want to know. The sun beat down on us, white and burning, but that coldness was creeping under my skin again. I spread my fingers hard on the edge of the stall.

"The doll way in back was saying something about the moon and lightning . . ."

"And about a flower, and death . . . that was the worst." Pollux said. "The flower and death part."

"And then another one, the one with the yellow hair that we threw the paint . . ." Pollux stopped and I knew he'd been talking about Derek and that they were for sure the ones who'd splashed the paint all over him and who'd done the other stuff, too. I wanted to face him with that, with what he'd just said, but I couldn't interrupt him now. Not when he was telling me about the dolls.

Castor shivered. "Anyway, the one with yellow hair by the path said 'Goodnight' in this creaky, croaky kind of voice. It freaks me out just thinking about it."

"He said '*Sweet* goodnight,' that's what he said," Pollux corrected. "Get it right."

"O.K. Sweet goodnight. But it still freaks me out."

My teeth were clenched so tightly my jaw hurt and my fingers spread on the table had gone numb.

"And did you say goodnight back?" Kristin asked,

grinning. "I bet you did. You're such a dork, Pollux."

"I'm Castor, and I didn't say a word. I took off like a bat out of daylight. We all did."

In the silence a truck pulled in behind us and a woman got out and came over. "I'll take ten of those lemons. Here's a dollar."

Clay Greeley put the lemons in one of the plastic bags, took her dollar, and said, "Our oranges are very nice today, too, ma'am." Nice, polite, freckle-faced little pumpkin head Clay Greeley.

The woman shook her head. "I'm up to the gazoos in oranges of my own, but thanks anyway."

Clay put the money in a red wooden cigar box and said, "Come again."

The woman was gone and we were left standing in silence. I swallowed to get my voice under control. "So, if you think the dolls talk, stay away. Then you won't have to hear them. Come on, Kristin."

I swung around and almost stepped on Abby, who was right behind me holding the rabbit. "Can I get it, please, Matt? Please, please. It's two dollars."

"I tell you what," Clay Greeley said before I could speak. "Because you're this nice guy's sister and to welcome you to the canyon, you can have it for free."

"Truly?" Abby was squirming, too happy to stand still. The bunny nestled against her neck. "Matt?"

"You can't have it, Ab. Put it back."

"But Matty . . ."

"Oh, he's so *mean*," one of the twins said. "He's mean to his little sister."

87

"Matty . . . can't I . . ."

"Put it back, Abby. Aunt Gerda didn't say we could bring home a rabbit. And besides . . ." Besides, I didn't want her taking anything from this guy, or buying anything either.

"We have to go right now, Abby," I said instead. I took the rabbit, settled it in the box, and put the screen back on top.

"You *are* mean," Ab whispered. "He said I could have it."

I grabbed her hand and pulled her toward the bike. "Well, I say you can't." This was all I needed, to have Ab start whining.

Behind us, I heard Kristin speaking to Clay Greeley. "So you're selling crystals now, too, Greeley. Thanks a lot. I really appreciate the competition."

Then Clay Greeley's voice. "All's fair in business, Kristin. And even if it wasn't . . ." I heard his laugh.

Abby kept her face turned from me as I lifted her into the bike seat.

"Listen," I whispered. "We'll ask Aunt Gerda, and if she says it's O.K., we'll get you a bunny somewhere else, all right?"

She kept her face turned away. "I wanted this one."

"Kid?" Clay Greeley called. "Little girl?" Abby looked back. "Don't worry about not taking the rabbit. If nobody buys him, my old man and me'll just put him in the stew pot."

Abby gasped and clutched at me. Her eyes were terrified. "He says . . ."

"I heard what he said. He's just trying to scare you. Don't listen to him, Ab."

I could hear their awful tittering as we rode away and I was filled with helpless rage. Clay Greeley had known I wouldn't let Ab take a rabbit from him and he'd known telling her about the stew would scare her to death. He'd like doing something like that . . .

Kristin was still yelling back at Greeley. "Remember the time I beat you up in school, Clay Greeley? Do you want me to do it again?"

"Aw, Kristin, you're scaring me. I *let* you hit me the last time 'cause I'm so polite. Next time I'm going to forget you're a girl."

Abby was whimpering and gulping in the seat behind me. As soon as we got around the bend in the road I stopped, lifted her down, and knelt beside her. Kristin stopped, too.

"Ab." I said. "I'm sorry you couldn't have the bunny. But those boys aren't nice. Kristin and I think they're the ones who did the bad things to Aunt Gerda's dolls."

"She wouldn't want you to take a bunny from them," Kristin added.

Tears rolled down Abby's face. "But he's going to *kill* it."

"No, he's not," Kristin said. "He's not going to kill anything he can sell for two dollars. Not Clay Greeley."

"Come on, Ab," I said. "Let's go home and see the dollies."

There was a stream of traffic now and we walked single file, pushing the bikes, Abby in the middle, me in front.

"So now we know for sure that they did it," Kristin said. "He just about admitted it. And all that baloney about the dolls talking. Did you ever . . . ?"

I stopped her with a nod down at Ab, who scuffed along with her head bent, her fingers in her mouth.

"I guess you sell crystals?" I asked Kristin in a light, ordinary voice.

"Yeah. Kristin's crystals. My dad and I find them when we hike back into the mountains. Then I purify them with fire and water so they have good vibes. I'm going to give you one, Abby, a rose quartz. They're pretty, all sparkly like diamonds."

Ab took her fingers out of her mouth. "A fire and water one?" she asked with interest.

"Sure."

I stared back at Kristin. "You *purify* them?"

Kristin winked. "Dad told me the tourists would go for that and he was right. They sell great. 'Course, now Clay Greeley's getting to the tourists first. What did you think of him, Matt?"

"He's sick," I said.

A string of motorcycles was passing, throttles open, motors roaring. Kristin raised her voice over the noise. "My mom says we have to excuse him for what he is. His dad drinks a lot and he's never there. Clay's mom died when he was real little so there's nobody . . ." She stopped and gave me a quick, apologetic glance.

"It's O.K.," I said. "And you don't have to be a creep just because your mother died."

"I know that."

It was too noisy now to talk, but not to think and I didn't want to think. All that stuff about the dolls talking. Clay and the twins were making it up, of course. But what strange words they'd heard the dolls say. Were they smart enough for that? And hadn't I heard the dolls myself, or thought I'd heard them?

I stopped, grabbed Ab's shoulder so she wouldn't step out into traffic, and faced Kristin . . . "I have to ask you something. Have *you* ever heard the D-O-L-L-S T-A-L-K?"

I spelled out the last two words and Abby swung around and beat my stomach with her fists. "I hate it when you do that, Matt. What did you say? Tell me."

I held both her little fists in one hand. "Quit it, Ab."

"No. I never heard the D-O-L-L-S T-A-L-K," Kristin said, spelling, too. "Because D-O-L-L-S can't T-A-L-K. O.K.?"

"I hope not," I said. "Because if these do, we're in big trouble."

"And if you start believing they do, *you're* in very big trouble," Kristin said.

Right then I wasn't sure what I believed.

9

I'D TOLD Clay Greeley I wouldn't be sleeping at all tonight and I'd meant it, because then I'd been determined to take my turn outside. But Aunt Gerda had refused my offer and settled herself on the porch instead. And man, was I glad. The thought of the dolls standing in the darkness talking to each other was enough to turn my bones to mush. Still, I set my alarm again for three. Every night that Aunt Gerda sat up I'd go down and be with her for a while. That I'd do. And I'd make the hot chocolate and bring it out to her. It wouldn't be so bad, I told myself. I wouldn't be alone.

So when something woke me, I thought it must be the alarm, and through my sleep I felt for the clock on the floor beside my cot. It wasn't ringing, though, and when I held it close to my eyes, I saw that it was only twenty minutes after one. What had wakened me, then? Something. What? I was getting used to the way my heart could start hammering for no reason at all.

I lay listening. Nothing but Abby's soft little snores. But something was wrong, something was missing. Then I knew what it was. There was only silence. Where were the crickets? Why wasn't the owl hooting its monotonous, hollow hoot? Had they taken the night off?

I got up, went cautiously to the door, and opened it. The stairs and the house below were filled with light. When I crouched, I could see the bottom part of the screen door to the porch and the light shining in from there, too. I could also see the little curve of the front tire of my bike that I'd propped at the side. Aunt Gerda gave a short rustle of a cough. Nothing wrong. Nothing to worry about.

I crossed to the window. Before we got into bed, I'd closed the blue curtains and now I tugged them open. The back yard was dark, with just the shaft of white light from the front lying across the vegetable garden, touching the side of the shed. What? I put my face against the glass, then raised the window so I could see better. Was the shed door open? It couldn't be, surely. Didn't Aunt Gerda keep it locked?

I stood, biting my knuckles, trying to think. What was in the shed that anybody would want? Not the rusted, broken-down lawnmower. The bike wasn't there anymore. Maybe the tools. The doll? The thought of that half-finished doll filled me with dread. But why would anyone want to steal her? Why?

I put on my jeans and sneakers, checked on Ab, then went quietly down the stairs. From their stands, Bethlehem and George watched me. How come the dolls always seemed to be turned facing me? Why was I always looking at their fronts and not their backs?

"Quit staring, will you?" I muttered and hurried past them, outside.

Aunt Gerda smiled up at me from the rocker. "I thought you might come down, Matthew, and I'm sure I should scold you. But it's just so nice to see you and to know that you care about me. Sit down for a few minutes, dear."

She leaned forward and lifted a pair of pants off the other chair. "Kristin's mother sent these over with Slim. She was quite right. They will be perfect for George."

I hovered, uncertain. The night air was cool on my bare chest, the sweat cold on my forehead.

"Aunt Gerda . . . I was going to come anyway, but . . . something woke me and when I looked out the back . . . I think the door to the shed is open. Did you leave it that way?"

"No."

The crickets were chirping again, filling the night with their racket. Did crickets stop singing when someone walked close to their homes in the long grass or the zucchini plants? Had someone been out there? Clay Greeley with his hard, cold eyes? The long, pale heavenly twins? Or maybe the vigilante leader, Gene Terlock, tired of businesslike methods, ready to scare Aunt Gerda out any way he could.

Aunt Gerda stood. The pea coat had been loosely round her shoulders and now she put her arms through the sleeves and buttoned it. I hadn't noticed the flashlight by the side of the chair till she picked it up and turned it on. We certainly weren't going to see much by its light. The battery should have been changed months ago. "Matthew, I want you to stay here. I'm going to go back to the shed and check."

"I'm going with you," I said. "No way are you going there alone." I thought she was about to argue and I couldn't help wishing she would. But then she said, "Very well. Just lock up. I have a key."

She waited while I clicked the front door closed and tried the knob, then went down the porch steps ahead of me. In the shadowy garden beyond the lights the dolls stood very still. I heard the faint creak as one of them turned on its pole, the faint creak as it swung back. Oh, boy, I thought. Now's the time for a dog, if ever there was a time, a big toothy dog that could leap ahead of us in the darkness. If only we had a dog, or a great heavy club, or . . . One of the Morton Salt signs had fallen across the grass and I picked it up. The top part looked like a rusted tin flag. The bottom was a sturdy stick with a pointed end. It rattled as I carried it and Aunt Gerda looked back at me, saw it, and nodded her approval.

We were round the side of the house now, the pale spot of the flashlight moving like a torn spiderweb in front of us. Aunt Gerda raised the beam and I saw the shed, the darkness inside the half-open door. The door creaked as she pushed it all the way back. "Who's in here?" she asked.

Only silence answered us.

She stepped forward. I stepped behind her, scuffing through the sawdust on the floor. If I'd been brave, I'd have gone ahead, carrying my Morton Salt banner pointed forward like a lance. O.K., I wasn't brave. I made myself small behind Aunt Gerda's bigness, peering around her as the faint light poked into the shed. The tin flag on the end of my lance rattled and I tried to steady it with both hands, felt it shake even more as I saw the empty, bare workbench, the sheet in a bundle on the ground. Iris was gone.

Aunt Gerda gave a little groan, ran forward, picked up the sheet, and held it to her face. The flashlight was smothered against her and I took it and made it jump in all directions. There was no one here.

"Do you think someone stole her?" I whispered. "Or did she . . . ?" Did she what? Get up and go for a night walk on her own? Get real, Matt. She wasn't even a she yet, just a lump of timber.

"Who would take her? Who would do such a thing?" Aunt Gerda's voice was strong and harsh.

I wanted to say that I knew who, or suspected anyway, and that it was probably done to be mean, to hurt, to take the heart out of her. Instead, I moved the beam of the flashlight in the direction of the windows. One had been pushed up and hung at a cockeyed angle on its cords. There was a gap of about twelve inches at the bottom, enough for someone to crawl through, maybe someone pale and sickly and skinny. I saw the white gouged-out wounds at the bottom of the old wood. It had been forced open against the lock. The someone had come in, taken Iris, opened the door, and walked out with her. She'd been too bulky to fit through that twelve-inch opening, so he'd made it easy for himself.

Aunt Gerda was striding toward the window and I hurried after her. "Isn't there a light in here?" I whispered.

"There is. I took the bulb for the house a long time ago."

I gave her the flashlight and she shone it through the opening. On the path below lay an iron bar. "Maybe there'll be fingerprints on that," I said. "We can take it to the police." And I thought, when they hear what's missing, they'll probably have a good laugh. Missing blocks of wood are not very high on their crime list.

The flashlight beam drifted around the outside yard, tangled in the grass, shimmied along the shine of the clothesline, and then Aunt Gerda gave a gasp, so filled with horror and pain that my heart lurched.

"What?" I whispered. "What is it? Do you see someone?"

"Oh, no," she said. "Oh, no."

Then she was pushing past me, going fast, taking the flashlight and leaving me alone in the darkness, still saying "Oh, no, oh, no."

I scurried after her. Don't leave me here. I don't like the dark. I don't like this place. Where was she going anyway? Not back to the house, down toward the bottom of the garden. Damp bits of things stuck themselves against my legs as I followed. My tin flag shook and rattled. A snail shell crunched under my shoe and some part of my mind recorded that the crickets were quiet again, lying hidden, listening to us blundering through the night. My elbow bumped the swing seat, sending it swaying backward into the darkness. "Ouch," I said. "That hurt."

And then I saw the hole in the ground where the grave had been, the earth mounded carelessly on one side, the white cross still standing straight. HERE LIES HARRIETTE, DEARLY BELOVED DAUGHTER . . . But not anymore.

"Oh, no," I whispered, like an echo of Aunt Gerda. "Oh, no."

Harriette was gone, too.

10

I GOT AUNT GERDA inside and upstairs and then went to make her hot chocolate. When I came back with it, she was in bed and I sat in the big chair under Uncle Joseph's photograph, letting her be quiet, letting the shaking stop. If only mine would stop. There's something about a grave, disturbed, dug up, that is unholy, even though it's just a doll's grave. And to Aunt Gerda it was worse. That was her child in there, her Harriette.

The clock by her bed ticked louder than my heartbeats. I put down my empty cup.

"Would you like me to leave now so you can sleep? I'll stay out on the porch for a while if you want."

"Thank you, Matthew, but the damage is done. They went in back while I watched in front. They got what they wanted. I don't think they'll come again. Not tonight."

"Will you be all right?"

"Yes. And I think I need to be alone for a while. Goodnight, dear Matthew."

"Goodnight."

I tucked her up the way she'd tucked us up every night since we'd come. She wore what looked like men's pajamas with the sleeves rolled up. The pins were out of her hair and it spread, gray and loose, on the pillow. On the very top there was a little bald spot that you couldn't see when she had it piled up. That bald spot almost did me in and I felt tears in my throat. How could they do this to her? I hated them, *hated* them. Hadn't I warned that Clay Greeley to stay away? He was going to get it now, all right.

"Try to sleep," I whispered to Aunt Gerda. "And we'll find Harriette and Iris . . ."

"Iris?" she asked wearily.

"The part-finished . . ."

"Oh, you mean Isadora."

"Yes. We'll find them both," I said and tiptoed out.

Before I got into the cot, I pulled our bedroom curtains tight again and then lay down, listening to the crickets. The watch crickets. Let them stop chirping and I'd be up in a flash. I closed my eyes, but opened them again when the pictures began coming behind my lids. The heavenly twins digging, pulling Harriette up from the earth, dirt falling from her like drops of water.

Or maybe she'd been in a coffin. Probably. Aunt Gerda and Uncle Joseph wouldn't have just opened a hole and tossed her in. He'd have made the coffin out there in the shed, cutting the wood, hammering the nails the way they did in old Western movies. So the twins and Greeley would have taken the coffin up and opened it, just to make sure that Harriette was inside. Her happy face would have smiled up at them because even when a doll died, it would still smile, wouldn't it? Now I was seeing Gene Terlock leaning on the spade, his thin lips stretched in a lizard grin. I hoped he or the twins got heart attacks on the spot.

Thinking about the dead Harriette almost gave me a heart attack myself. Were her eyes open or closed? I curled myself small and cocooned the blanket around me. Greeley and the twins probably carried the coffin along the road on their shoulders the way Mr. Valdoni and Mr. Norvis and Archie Schultz and I had carried Mom's. What had they done with Isadora? Tied her on top? If it was Mr. Terlock, he could have put them in his car. Would a coffin fit in a car? But I hadn't heard any car . . .

I jammed my fist against my eyes to stop the thoughts coming, but they wouldn't stop. Sometime I slept, but my dreams were bad, too, and I was glad when Abby woke me to morning and sunlight.

"Can we ask Aunt Gerda about the rabbit?" she demanded right away.

"Not today, Ab," I said.

"But why?"

"Because Aunt Gerda isn't feeling well. And besides, isn't Kristin bringing over the crystal for you?"

"Oh, yeah! That's right. I didn't know she was bringing it today."

"She said she would."

I decided it must be pretty nice to be only five and easily distracted.

Sometime in the middle of the night I'd realized that I should get up early and fill in Harriette's grave so Aunt Gerda wouldn't have to look at it and Abby wouldn't see it. But when I went outside, I found Aunt Gerda had already done it.

She seemed calm enough as she mixed water and powdered milk in a pitcher, but I saw the twitch in one of her eyes and noticed how her hands trembled. Poor Aunt Gerda. Poor doll mother.

Kristin came after eleven. She'd wrapped the crystal in green tissue paper and I let her give it to Ab before I told her what had happened in the night.

"So what are you going to do about it?" she demanded, facing me angrily with her hands on her hips.

"Something," I said vaguely, as if I didn't know. But I did know and I knew when. This time, though, Kristin wasn't going to be in on it. Aunt Gerda was my aunt. This was my cause.

"I swear, Matt O'Meara," Kristin began in a disgusted voice, "if you *don't*, you're . . ."

I interrupted her. "Kristin? Could you tell me how Harriette died?" Aunt Gerda had said, "I don't want to talk about it in front of the children," so I lowered my voice and turned my head in case the dolls could read lips.

"Harriette was shot," Kristin said. "Shot first, and now kidnapped. It's not fair."

I picked up my Morton Salt sign and rammed the point into the wooden step. "Shot? By Greeley?"

"No."

"By one of the vigilantes?"

"No. It was back a while, about six years ago, when there was still hunting up here in the canyon. Two guys with rifles drank too much beer and they wandered down here and shot up a bunch of stuff."

Kristin looked up and pointed and I saw that a tin C AND H SUGAR sign tacked to the wall had a rusted hole through the middle. "There used to be a weathervane on top of the house, a rooster crowing. I can sort of remember it. They shot that, too, and then, well, one of them shot Harriette. Three times."

"But did it matter? Couldn't Uncle Joseph take the bullets out and patch her up? I mean, she isn't human."

"One went through her heart, one went through her lungs, one went in her leg," Kristin said solemnly.

"But she didn't *have* a heart or lungs. I can see the *leg*, but . . ."

"Joseph and Gerda believed she had. And how do you know she hadn't?"

"Because she was a doll," I said. "Give me a break, Kristin."

Kristin shrugged. "You asked how she died and I told you."

I glanced across at the dolls and I could have sworn they were all leaning toward us, trying to hear.

Kristin jumped up. "I have piano practice. If I don't go home, Mom'll kill me."

"Thanks for bringing the crystal for Abby," I said.

"That's O.K." Kristin hesitated. "We are going to do something about this, aren't we, Matt?"

"I'm thinking about it," I said. I was thinking about nothing else.

Sometimes Abby refuses to take a nap. I hoped it wouldn't be that way today because today I was going to break my word to her, my promise to never leave her alone. While she slept, I was going to go to Clay Greeley's. If Harriette and Isadora were there, I'd bring them back somehow.

I left as soon as Abby fell asleep. Aunt Gerda was sitting at the kitchen table adding columns of figures in a red ledger. George and Bethlehem stood behind, as if reading over her shoulder. Crikes! George was wearing reading glasses!

"I . . . I didn't know George wore glasses," I said.

Aunt Gerda put a finger on the page to hold her place and turned around. "He doesn't usually. Abigail found those in one of the bags and I'm really glad. They'll make it easier for him. His eyes have been looking a little weak lately."

I wanted to say "The paint's fading," but I didn't.

There were things I couldn't say to Aunt Gerda.

"Well, I'm going to ride," I told her. "Will you listen for Ab? I'll try to be back before she wakes up."

"Enjoy the sunshine, Matthew. And take your time."

The canyon was quieter today, with only the birds chirping at me from the trees and the small hum of the telephone wires. There was a smell of honeysuckle in the air. But I was in no mood to enjoy any of it. I rode faster than fast so I'd have no time to get more nervous than I was already, and in case I tried to change my mind and chicken out on this. That was possible. With every minute I could feel part of my fierceness ebbing away. Was I rushing into this too fast? After all, I wasn't certain about anything. Maybe I needed to think this out some more. I slowed down, but I got to the house too quickly anyway.

Clay's stall was gone from the yard and without it the old, tumbledown place looked worse than it had before. I rang the doorbell twice, but no one came, not even when I banged on the wood. The front window was so dirty I couldn't see anything through it even though I put my face up close to the glass. I banged on it, too, before I let myself realize that there was nobody home.

"Shoot," I said under my breath. "Now what?" And I tried not to admit that I was more relieved than disappointed. The door was locked when I tried the handle.

"Locked," I said out loud. "Wouldn't you know?" I

was feeling better all the time. I'd tried, hadn't I? That was all anybody could expect. I'd even try some more.

I walked around the side of the house. The stall was there, placed neatly against the back wall, still set up the way it had been on Sunday, with its crates of lemons and avocados and bags of oranges. The cardboard signs were stacked flat. They'd just carried everything around here, and I guessed that next week they'd carry everything back.

In a netting wire cage was the rabbit. I poked a finger through the mesh and he sniffed cautiously at it with his soft nose. "Hi," I said. "Hi, rabbit." Someone had given him fresh water and there was a stub of carrot poked through the netting. So he hadn't gone in the stew pot after all. Kristin had been right. Next weekend he'd probably be out in front, for sale again, too.

I walked all the way to the scrubby back hedge, kicking a path for myself through the rotted plums. Ants crawled over my shoes and up my legs. There was no place to hide Harriette or Isadora out here. They had to be inside and I couldn't get inside. I'd have to come back some other time.

And then I saw the open back door to the house. It hung on broken hinges, inviting me inside. Maybe I hesitated for ten seconds, thinking about breaking and entering or whatever it's called when you go into somebody's house without their permission. Whatever it was, it had to be against the law. But look what

Clay Greeley had done last night, I told myself. That was against the law, too, and a heck of a lot worse than just taking a quick look inside the house. I decided there was no way I could wimp out of this and feel O.K. about myself. So I edged through the door.

The inside back porch was filled with old boots and shovels and gardening tools. I picked up one of the shovels and examined it. The blade was thick with dirt. This could be the one they used to dig up Harriette, I thought. But there was no way to be sure.

The small living room was the grungiest room I'd ever seen and the kitchen was worse. Pans of yellow scummy water sat on the floor. I figured they'd been there since it had rained, catching the drips from the leaky roof. Flies buzzed around pans and plates gummy with food. One glance told me that neither Harriette nor Isadora was here either.

The smell in the bedroom almost made me gag, but I forced myself to go in, to pull down the stained sheet and blanket on the tumbled bed in case the dolls were beneath them. No dolls. I yanked a pile of dirty clothes from underneath the bed, poked them back in. I checked through the mess in the closet. Nothing.

I was rushing now, trying to figure how long I'd been here, knowing I was in an inside room with no way out if Clay Greeley or his father came back. I'd be trapped. And what reason could I give for being in the bedroom? In the living room I could maybe bluff something, but not in here.

At the far end of the room was a blue curtain on a pole. My heart was chug-a-lugging the way it does when I start to panic. I didn't want to take the time to look behind the curtain. I wanted out of here, now and fast. But suppose the dolls were back there? What was the sense of leaving without checking?

I hurried across, rattled the curtain open on its rings, and stood staring. Behind was a single bed and a small wooden chest of drawers. The bed was smoothly and perfectly made, the way I guess a bed in an army barracks would be, with the sheets crisp and white and knife edged, and the corners folded in, neat as envelopes. There wasn't a wrinkle or a bulge. No need to check if the dolls were in *that* bed. They weren't.

The top of the dresser was bare except for a picture of a sad-looking lady in a cheap plastic frame and two pieces of purple crystal that could have been the ones I'd seen on the stall on Sunday. Those drawers were way too shallow to hold the dolls. I turned back toward the other bedroom and looked into the depressing, disgusting mess. Then I pulled the curtain, shutting myself in the corner. This was Clay Greeley's space. I knew it. The only place he could find for himself in this yuck of a house. Maybe he'd tired of all of it and given up. After his mother died? After his dad started drinking?

Some feeling of pity trailed inside of me, but I pushed it away. What did I care about how hard things were for Clay Greeley? He'd still been rotten enough to do what he did last night, and the other times, too. I jerked up the bed cover and bent to look underneath. Nothing but bare, clean boards and a sharp smell of disinfectant. I was just about to straighten up when I saw the edge of red beneath the dresser. Whatever it was had been pushed well back and it was hard to reach, but I got it out. The Indian Head cigar box that Clay Greeley had used for his cash yesterday on the stall. Should I open it? If he'd hidden it this carefully, there might be more inside than money, a clue maybe, something.

I opened the lid. Inside were dollar bills, neatly stacked, and a pile of quarters and dimes. I picked up the bills and ruffled through them. In the middle, with four singles on top and five beneath were six fifties. Three hundred dollars! Where would Clay Greeley get that kind of money? And in fifties? Not from selling oranges and lemons and avocados. Not from crystals, either, I was pretty sure. So where?

There was something else here, too, folded in the bottom of the box. It was an ad clipped from a magazine. PACKAGE DEAL, it said. WANT PEACE AND QUIET? AIR YOU CAN BREATHE? SOLITUDE YOU CAN TOUCH? BUY YOUR LAND IN BEAUTIFUL WASHINGTON STATE. BUILD YOUR OWN LOG CABIN. IT COSTS LESS THAN YOU THINK. CALL US.

There was an area code and a phone number. The paper was almost worn through at the creases and I could tell it had been handled a lot. I folded it, put it back with the money on top, and slid the box under the dresser again. Peace, quiet, solitude.

I had too much to think about, too much to puzzle over, but not here. Not in this dangerous room in this dangerous house.

I left the way I'd come in, grabbed my bike, and put plenty of space between me and the Greeleys' place before I slowed. And all the time my legs were pumping my brain was pumping, too. Had somebody paid Greeley to hassle Aunt Gerda? Gene Terlock? But why? Because he was too much of a businessman to do it himself? Plots from books I'd read and TV movies I'd seen jumbled around in my head. The land was valuable, not just nicely situated in the canyon. There was gold in the ground, or oil.

But if Clay Greeley had taken the dolls, where were they? At the twins' house? Of course Clay could have dumped them. I imagined the two dolls floating through the night in some dark river, Harriette's drowned face, water bubbling up through the bullet holes in her heart and lungs, and I wished I didn't have such a good imagination.

11

AUNT GERDA was sitting on the porch when I got back. I asked her if Ab was still napping and she said yes, so I flopped down in the other chair beside her. She looked terrible and I wished more than ever that I could have found Harriette and Isadora and brought them back for her.

"I bet you're real tired," I said, pulling off my Mariners cap, fanning myself with it. "Would you like me to rub your neck? I'm pretty good at that. Mom used to like it."

Aunt Gerda gave me one of her nice smiles. "Thank you, Matthew. But I don't think a neck rub's going to help today." She picked up an envelope that lay on the table. "This just came." It was from the Water and Power Department and the note inside said that unless the bill was paid in full in the next three days, all the utilities would be shut off. The bill was for $364.22.

"Three hundred sixty-four dollars and twenty-two cents," I gasped. "That's so much. There must be a mistake. I used to write our checks for Mom, you know, at the end, and our electric bill was about twenty-five dollars. In fact, didn't you send us money once to pay?" She had sent it one month when we were going to have our electricity disconnected. I remembered perfectly.

"This one's for four months," Aunt Gerda said, her left eye twitching. "And I can't blame them. They've given me lots of warnings."

"You don't have the money?" I asked hesitantly, afraid to hear her answer.

"No. I'm not even close."

We sat quietly rocking while I tried to think.

"Ab and I have a hundred and thirty-eight dollars," I said. "You can have that and . . ."

"Matthew," Aunt Gerda sat forward in her chair. "I feel bad that I asked you and little Abigail to come here. It was irresponsible, things being the way they are. I just couldn't bear to think of you two going into some place . . . maybe being separated. Your mother loved you so. Children shouldn't be separated. But I'm sorry I brought you into the middle of this."

"Don't say that," I told her. "Your letter was the only good thing we had when Mom died. We were so scared."

She went on as if talking to herself, as if she hadn't heard me. "I don't know why I'm always such an optimist. I thought we'd muddle through." She swept a hand around the yard at the ever-smiling dolls.

They're optimists, for sure, I thought. Grinning and smirking as if everything's O.K.

"The children and I don't need much," Aunt Gerda said. "I expect we could do without electricity. People did in the old days. We don't miss the phone at all. In fact, we're better off without all those hateful calls. But I'm not sure if we could do without water, and of course, what would happen to the freezer? A lot of the food we use is in there."

She looked directly at me and I saw that her eye was still twitching. "And, Matthew, if we have no lights to turn on, they'll come when it's dark, and take the rest of the children the way they took Harriette and Isadora."

"No, they won't. We'll stop them. We'll get candles and lamps."

Her gaze was fixed somewhere on the sky above the trees. "I've nothing left to sell, Matthew."

"Wait," I said, excited suddenly. "We have Mom's paintings. Sure. When Mr. Stengel comes . . ."

"You're a kind, loving boy. But I'm not sure the paintings would bring in enough money to save us. And besides, I wouldn't want you to give up what you have left from your mother . . . not for me."

"For all of us," I said. "This is our home now, too. You said that. And Mom would want us to. She would." What did Aunt Gerda mean, anyway, that the paintings wouldn't bring in enough money? Of course they would. We had just three days to sell them. Three days. I'd have to get going on it right away.

"I think I'll go up and see if Ab's awake," I said and went upstairs.

Abby wasn't, but she rubbed her eyes and smiled at me when I spoke her name. It kills me the way Ab smiles first thing like that. No wonder Mom called her Sunshine.

I opened the portfolio and laid the paintings edge to edge along the cot and on the bottom of Ab's bed. The colors glowed in the sunlight, the blues, the reds, the yellow and browns of Mom's *Woods in Autumn*, which was nothing but leaves splattered in a vivid blaze across the canvas. We'd gone to Blake's Glen that day, the three of us, with a picnic. It was before Mom got so sick, while she could still do things. I'd carried the picnic bag and our jackets, because it had gotten so warm we'd had to take them off. Mom had her paints and easel and canvas, and Ab blundered along, wading through the leaves clutching Sweetie Pie, her old bald-headed doll, and the tartan blanket that had gone with us on so many picnics.

Looking at the painting now I could smell the dry, peppery dead-leaf smell and hear the crunch as they crumbled under my feet. There was a little river and we'd sat on sun-warmed rocks and dabbled our feet in water that was clear as ice. Ab had dropped Sweetie Pie and screamed when the doll began spiraling downstream, and I'd had to wade in deep to get her. The remembrance of Sweetie Pie changed, turned into Harriette in another unknown river. I shivered. No, don't think about Harriette, don't let thoughts of her float into the good memories.

I set *Woods in Autumn* aside. "We won't sell this one."

Ab pointed at the painting of Tetley, Mrs. Valdoni's dog, asleep at the bottom of the apartment house stairs. "And not this one, either. Where's the one of you and me?"

"Here." I put it on the "keep" pile.

Ab looked at the framed picture on the wall. "And that one's Aunt Gerda's."

"Yes."

"And not Mom's picture of herself, huh, Matty? We'll keep that one for ever and ever, won't we?"

"For ever and ever."

I slid the other paintings back in the portfolio.

"Who's going to buy them, Matty? Will we get this much money?" Ab spread her arms wide.

"I hope so." I buckled the straps, then took Abby's spread-apart hands. "Listen, Ab. This is a secret, yours and mine. Aunt Gerda might try to stop us selling the pictures if she knew."

"Why?"

"Because she thinks we're selling them to give *her* the money, and in a way we are. But it's for us, too. It'll be such a great surprise for her. So don't spoil it, O.K.?"

"O.K."

"That means you, too, Teddy," I told him. "Not a word."

Abby hadn't even asked how we were going to do this wonderful thing and I wasn't sure myself. But I knew I would. And when I'd told Ab it was for us as well as Aunt Gerda, I'd meant it. This was our home, too—the only one we had. No one else was going to get it.

I stayed behind when she went downstairs and I found the card Mr. Stengel had given me and slipped it and some change into my pocket.

"I thought I'd ride Ab and me in to take a look at the village," I told Aunt Gerda. "How far is it?"

Aunt Gerda was fixing red earrings in Cleo's ears, and she said, "Excuse me a minute, Cleo" before she turned to answer me. "About two miles."

"You don't need me for anything?"

"Nothing."

I'd just noticed that Cleo's ears were pierced. Unbelievable!

Abby stopped stringing red beads on a piece of thread to stare up at me, delighted.

"We're going someplace now? Are we going to . . "

I warned her with a finger on my lips.

"Can I bring Teddy?" she asked.

"Sure. But let's go."

She tried again on the way out. "Aunt Gerda? Me and Matt have a terrific secret."

"You do?"

"Ah," I said. 'We're *going. Now.*"

"You're really good at keeping secrets," I told her as I lifted her onto the bicycle seat.

"I know," she said.

The front door of Clay Greeley's house was open as we passed. Someone was home. Clay, maybe. Did he carry his meals in behind that curtained corner? Did he count his money? Did he read his leaflet on how to build a log cabin and dream of going somewhere clean where he could breathe? Or did he sit in there, smiling that horrible smile, thinking of how clever he'd been to steal Harriette and Isadora? I gritted my teeth. That was more likely. If only he knew, nobody needed to hassle Aunt Gerda, not him, not the vigilantes, not anyone. The bills were going to drive her out sooner or later.

I spotted an Esso gas station with two wall phones right on the road, close to town.

"You watch the bike and hold Teddy," I told Ab and fished Mr. Stengel's card from my pocket.

"Are you calling Mrs. Valdoni?" Ab asked.

"No."

"Who, then?"

"Give me a break, will you?"

I was dialing now, listening to the phone ring.

It was a woman who answered. "Black Orchid Gallery."

"Mr. Stengel, please."

117

"I'm sorry, he isn't in today. May I take a message?"

"Oh, no. I'm a friend of his and he told me to call. When will he be back?"

"I expect him tomorrow, around noon. Would you like to leave your name, sir?"

I thought I heard her smile in the way she said that "sir," as if she knew I wasn't as grown-up as I was trying to sound.

"That's O.K.," I said. "I'll come in tomorrow at noon."

Black Orchid Gallery, La Cienega Boulevard, Los Angeles. Where the heck *was* that? It might as well be on the moon for all I knew.

I pushed the bike over to where a mechanic in greasy overalls was working with his head stuck inside the open hood of a car and Ab skipped along beside me.

"Excuse me. Could you tell me how to get to La Cienega Boulevard?"

He didn't move and his voice came up muffled from the depths of the motor. "No such place around here."

"Yes, there is." I tried to poke Mr. Stengel's card down in front of his eyes.

His head turned and he looked up at me. "You're talking L.A."

"Yes."

When he straightened, I saw he had HENRY in red stitching on the pocket of the coveralls. He eyeballed me good, then said: "Are you kids planning on riding bicycles down there?" I guess this guy was what people mean when they say "deadpan." His face, his lips, didn't move as he talked and he was slow, slow, slow. Mrs. Valdoni would have said the dead fleas were dropping off him.

"It's probably too far to ride," I said. "How can we get there?"

"You could rent a limo."

He didn't smile, but I guessed he was joking. "Seriously," I said.

Henry gave me back the card with his big, greasy thumbprint in the middle of it. "You'd take a bus into L.A. and transfer." He jerked his head toward a glass cubicle with OFFICE printed above it. "Come on inside."

There was a big city map tacked on the wall and Henry stood considering it. I saw the crisscrossings of freeways and streets.

"Here's La Cienega."

My heart flopped. Never in a million years would Ab and I be able to find our way there.

"Here's how you do her." His finger made the trip again. "You're not planning on going, just the two of you?"

"No," I said. "We'll have somebody with us." And I thought, we'll have Teddy. Ab won't leave *him* behind.

"O.K., then." Henry tore a piece of paper off a yellow pad and wrote a bunch of stuff, looking back and forth at the map.

"The L.A. bus leaves this corner every day at ten minutes past the hour," he said, giving me the paper. "I've put down what to ask when you get to the terminal, and you'd better take this." He rummaged around in a drawer and pulled out a folded Los Angeles County map.

"Thanks a lot."

"I have a bunch of bus schedules somewhere, too." He found them and gave me one. "Are you kids new around here?" he asked. "I don't recall seeing you before. Where do you live?"

"With our Aunt Gerda and the children," Ab said.

Henry's deadpan face didn't change. "You mean, you're living out in the Yourra house?"

I nodded. His eyes went from me to Ab and back.

"Little girl?" he asked, slow as pancake syrup. "Do you like gum?"

"Yeah," Abby breathed.

"Well, here." Henry fished in the pocket of his overalls and held a palm full of change toward Ab. "Take the pennies. There's a gumball machine over there. How about getting a few pieces for everybody?"

Abby picked out the pennies with greedy little fingers. She never once looked at me and I knew why. She loves gum and she was afraid I'd stop her. I'm on to Ab's little tricks. But I didn't say anything because I had a feeling Henry was getting her out of the way for some reason and that I ought to know for what.

"I don't like the idea of you two kids out in that

house," he said softly as Ab ran for the gum machine. "That Mrs. Yourra's real strange and . . ."

"She's O.K.," I said.

"Maybe she's not the one I'm worrying about," Henry went on.

"You're worried about the dolls? Everybody is, but . . ."

He held up a hand. "I'm not saying I'm not worried about them and that you shouldn't be. There's something not right about those dolls. But I'm talking now about practical things. The canyon people want rid of your aunt and there's some that would go to just about any lengths to get her to leave."

"You think I don't *know* that? Criminy . . . that Mr. Terlock . . ."

"Do you know someone tried to burn her out a year or so ago? Slim Ericson was passing and saw smoke and got the house wet down till the fire engines arrived. If it hadn't been for him, the whole place would have been ashes and your Aunt Gerda with it."

Beyond him I could see Ab working intently on the gum machine.

Henry kept on talking. "There was a big fuss because they found an empty gas can and I think the attention scared off whoever set the fire. But just a couple months back someone broke all her windows and when she came out, they threw a rock at her. It cut the side of her head."

I shivered. "Did they ever find out who did it?"

"No," Henry said.

Abby was coming back. She dropped two or three of the gumballs, picked them up, wiped them on her skirt.

Henry was watching her, too. "Look!" His deadpan voice speeded up. "If you get scared, if anything happens, call, O.K.?"

He stopped as Abby tugged at his arm. She held out the gumballs. "You take the red ones. They're the best and you can have them 'cause it's your money."

"You're sure it's not because these are the ones you dropped?" Henry asked.

"Uh-uh," Abby said, offended.

"Well, thank you, little girl."

"I'm not little girl. I'm Abby and he's Matt."

"We've got to go," I told Henry. "Thanks for the gum and the other stuff."

"I'm here just about all the time," he said.

"Thanks," I said again.

I helped Ab up onto the bike. Her hands were full of gumballs and I had to persuade her to let go of them and drop them in her pockets so she could hold on to me. Behind me I could hear her singing "Jingle Bells," happy as a lark. I was glad she hadn't heard.

In bed that night I studied Henry's directions, marked the route on the map, and checked the timetable. And I worried a lot. Suppose we did get to Mr. Stengel's studio? Suppose he did buy the paintings and we did get a lot of money, what then? The money could save Aunt Gerda and the house. And the children.

And forevermore we'd have to be on guard, the way we were now, because money wasn't going to change how the canyon people thought.

Henry's words kept coming back, however hard I tried to shut them out. I got out of bed and checked how far it would be for Ab and me to jump from the window if there was another fire. I should get a rope or see if there was a ladder and leave it outside against the wall. But a person could come up a ladder as well as down. A person could come while we were asleep, step over the windowsill into our room. I wondered if a thrown rock could hit us in bed. Would flying glass come through the curtains?

"Look after Abby," Mom had said. She'd wanted us to come to Aunt Gerda's, but she hadn't known how dangerous things were. Shootings, fires, rocks. Maybe I'd have to get Ab out of here. But the first thing was to sell the paintings. Without money I had no choices.

I went downstairs again at three because I'd promised myself I would.

"Abby and I didn't see much of the village yesterday," I told Aunt Gerda. "I think we'll go in again today."

She looked at me vaguely, then said: "Did I tell you Kristin came by? She said she'd be over in the morning. She said maybe you and Abigail would like to go crystal hunting with her."

"Oh." Should I put the trip off for another day? No. Every day here, every night, could be dangerous.

Around us and in front the lights blazed. If I looked into the dark, I could see the pale floss of Derek's hair and the sliced edge of his checkered pants.

"I love this canyon," Aunt Gerda said dreamily. "I've always loved it and soon I'll have to leave it."

I started to comfort her, to say "Maybe not," but the words wouldn't come. It would be better if she *did* leave. If we all left. All of us except the dolls. But would she go without them?

"At night, sitting out here, I think about Joseph and a time when we were young," she said softly. "We had such plans, the two of us. We'd have children, lots of children, and they'd run free, and we'd teach them about nature. For a time it seemed as if it wasn't to be and I have to admit that I took that hard."

The dolls moved gently on their poles, seemed to sigh along with the little wind. The steady roll of Aunt Gerda's rocker was as soothing as a lullaby.

"And then Joseph began making the children for me. First there was Arabella, and a pretty little thing she was. She was made from love. Joseph told me, and it was true, Matthew. It was true, but after we lost Harriette, the life seemed to go out of him, and then he started Isadora and, well, he died before she was finished, so I lost her, too. It's a great blessing that I have the others." Her hand came out briefly and touched mine. "And now I have you and little Abigail."

She'd never give up the dolls. There was no point in thinking that she would.

124

"Ah, well. Forgive me for being so mournful, Matthew. It's this time of morning. There's melancholy in the air. I shouldn't inflict it on you. I'll keep going as long as I can. All else is in God's hands."

I don't know how long we sat together, quietly, with just the sounds of the crickets around us. My eyelids were heavy and I thought that, worried or not, I'd be able to sleep. I was just wondering if I'd sat with Aunt Gerda long enough, if I could leave now, when she spoke again.

"Matthew? I have to go inside for just a minute. Would you mind being here with the children till I get back?"

"No. I don't mind. Go ahead."

"You're not afraid of the children, are you?" she asked gently.

"Of course not," I lied.

"I'm glad. Some people are, you know. They don't understand."

I nodded to show that I did, which was another lie.

"The children like you a lot," she said.

Oh, criminy! "They told you that?" I asked.

Aunt Gerda patted my shoulder. "They told me."

"Oh, well, good." For a minute I thought about standing up and shouting "Thanks, you guys." Maybe I was going nuts myself.

Aunt Gerda stepped down onto the path. "I'll be back in a few minutes, children," she said. "Matthew will be here."

"I'll be here," I echoed. See? I *was* going nuts.

When she went inside, I sat back in the chair, rocked, and tried to relax. A moth flapped itself too close to the hanging light bulb, retreated, flapped back.

"You turkey," I muttered. "Do you want to fry?"

Your Aunt Gerda would have been ashes, Henry had said. I rocked harder and hummed a little tune under my breath. She'd be back in a few minutes. No sweat.

I was glad, anyway, that she'd told me about Uncle Joseph and how he'd come to make the dolls. Then they'd both started pretending they were real. Easy to see how that could happen. They were ghost children, all right.

Something rustled in the tired shrubbery below the porch and I sat up, my heart pecking inside my chest. I thought I heard a click, like a gun being cocked. But that had to be my imagination, too. I'd be such an easy target here, under the light. I'd be a sitting duck. I scrunched down as far as I could go.

How long had Aunt Gerda been in there? More than a few minutes. Where in heck was she?

And then, plain as plain from the darkest part of the yard came a little girl's voice. "We like you a lot, Matthew."

This time I got out of the chair slowly, edged myself behind it.

"Did . . . did somebody say something?"

"We all like you a lot, Matthew." A boy's voice this time, high and babyish. "We like Abigail, too."

I backed against the house, staring into the darkness.

It wasn't my imagination, not this time. There was no one here except me and them. No way to reason myself around that one. The dolls had talked.

12

THE DOLLS had absolutely and definitely talked.

There's something not right about them, Henry had said in his deadpan way. He wasn't kidding. And neither were the twins; they'd heard the dolls, too.

Shootings, a fire, rocks, kidnapping, and now a bunch of dolls that talked like people. I couldn't stop shaking. The dolls talking had finished it for me. So what if they liked me? Ab and I were leaving.

Lying in bed, I made mental lists. First we'd need money. I'd go into the Black Orchid Gallery the way I'd planned, and when I'd sold the paintings, I'd give half to Aunt Gerda because we owed her a lot and because . . . well, just because. Was she a witch? Don't think about that, Matt. Don't think about it. I'd call the airport and book Ab and me on a flight to Seattle. I'd call Mrs. Valdoni, too. She'd take us in temporarily, till we got things together. We'd find a secret place, the two of us, where nobody could get to us or separate us. I remembered Clay Greeley's mountain cabin. How much would something like that cost? I'd fish and we'd have a garden like the one here, except there'd be no dead dolls buried in ours.

But first, the money.

When it began to get light outside, I heard Aunt Gerda come in, heard the door of the bathroom close behind her, and I grabbed Mom's portfolio and ran quickly downstairs with it. Curving wide, keeping as far from the dolls as I could, I hid it in high weeds by the hedge. Then I turned and said, "You guys?" My voice sounded like Jell-O. "I know you saw me do that, but don't tell her, O.K.? She'll try to stop me and I'm selling the paintings for all of us, for you guys, too. So keep your mouths shut."

Arabella's purse slipped from her shoulder to hang, swinging from her wrist, and I jumped at least six inches off the ground before I turned and raced for the front steps. Just let Ab and me get safely out of here. Safely and quickly.

There was instant oatmeal with canned peaches for breakfast. I glanced quickly at the glass case under the counter. Yep. This was the last can of peaches and Aunt Gerda was giving it to us. Witch or not, she was kind and good. Well, soon she'd have money. Soon she could buy herself a whole caseful of canned peaches.

"Ab," I said, "hurry up and finish. We're going for another bike ride this morning and I want to leave early."

"Do I have to go?" Abby got up and fished the last slice of peach from the can with her fingers. "Aunt Gerda's starting a new skirt for Cleo today. And she said Kristin's coming over. She'd going to show us where to find crystals. And I want to help make Cleo's skirt. You go, Matt. I'll stay."

That's right! Kristin was going to come. So? I couldn't worry about that. What I'd do was call her from Henry's gas station. But what was this baloney about Ab wanting to stay, without me? I could hardly believe what I was hearing. *Ab* was telling me to go somewhere and she'd stay. Little nervous Ab. And naturally it would be just at a time when I didn't want her to stay.

I told myself it was great that Ab was so much better. I'd wished for a long time that she'd stop clinging and hanging on to me, because that was no good for a little kid. But I felt a bit let down, too. This was the first time in two years that Abby hadn't wanted to be with me. Anyhow, she couldn't stay. It would be a while till Kristin got here. There was no way I was going to leave her behind with Aunt Gerda and the talking dolls. No way.

"You have to come," I said sharply. "So don't argue. Just go and wash your hands. You're not supposed to stick your fingers in the peach can. And wash your bowl and spoon while you're at it."

Aunt Gerda gave me an apologetic glance. "Abigail? When I told you last night you could help with Cleo's skirt and Kristin would be over, I didn't know

Matthew had other plans. Cleo's skirt can wait till to-morrow. That's all right, Cleo, isn't it?"

Don't answer, Cleo, please. Not in front of Ab.

"You and I will cut out the pattern when you get home, my dear," Aunt Gerda said. "And Kristin can take you to look for crystals any day, all summer long. Matthew really wants your company."

Abby gave me a doubtful glance. "Truly, Matty?"

"Truly," I said.

Ab smiled. "O.K."

The Ovaltine clock said ten minutes to eight when we left. Aunt Gerda was busy now washing down the front of the glass cases, so I didn't think she'd come out on the porch to see us off. Still, I was careful to check before I pulled the portfolio from its hiding place. All clear.

"Why did you hide Mom's paintings out here?" Ab asked in a loud voice. "Where are we taking . . ."

"Shh!" I said. "It's part of the secret. Remember?" I lifted her onto the seat of the bike and balanced the portfolio across the handlebars. Teddy was jammed inside my shirt with his furry head sticking up under my chin. He and the portfolio kept slipping, but I couldn't think of a better way to carry them.

"We're going to Los Angeles," I told Ab over my shoulder. "Remember Mr. Stengel? He might want to buy some of Mom's paintings."

"Oh, boy," Abby said. "Will he give us all the money today?"

"Could be."

"Oh, boy," Abby said again.

I didn't try to talk to Ab as we rode. The wheels of the bicycle sizzled and burned on the road, singing their own scary song: "We all like you a lot, Matthew, a lot, a lot." I pedaled harder.

Henry was in his little gas station office.

"We're on our way to the bus," I told him. "Can I leave the bike here till we get back?"

"Sure."

I tried to keep my eyes steady when I looked at him and push that tiny, little girl doll voice out of my head in case the memory would show and I'd turn into a lump of Jell-O again. "We like you a lot, Matthew. We like Abigail, too."

Henry made a big point of getting up and looking behind us. "I don't see that adult person who was supposed to be with you."

"It's different than I said. But I know what I'm doing."

He nodded, then slid a piece of paper toward me. "Write down where you're going on La Cienega." When I'd written it, he folded the paper and put it in his top pocket. "What time will you be back?"

"Three or four. It depends how long it takes."

"I guess this trip is important?"

"Yes." I fished a dollar bill out of my pocket. "Can you give me some change? I have to call somebody."

"Who?" Abby asked.

"Ab?" I asked. "How come you're always asking me who I'm calling? You don't have to know."

Henry grinned. "Why not use the phone in here? As long as it's a local call. Is it?"

"Yeah."

"Well, go ahead, then. Sis and I'll wait outside." He winked at Abby. "So he can be private. Big brothers need privacy sometimes, you know."

"Thanks," I said. I propped the portfolio against his desk, found the Ericson's number in his phone directory, and dialed.

It was Fee who answered and I had trouble getting him to go for Kristin. I guess little brothers can give you a hard time, too.

At last she came. "Hi," she said. "What's up? Where are you calling from, anyway?"

"From Henry's gas station," I said.

There was a long silence. "What are you doing there? I was just getting ready to ride over to Gerda's. Did she tell you I was coming?"

"Yes, but . . ."

"If you don't want to go find crystals, that's O.K. I thought Abby might like it. Maybe she'd still want to go."

"Ab's with me," I said.

Henry's desk was covered with a sheet of dirty glass. Underneath it he'd pushed business cards, ads for pizza, and pictures of baseball players. I ran my fingers around the outline of Fernando Valenzuela. "We have to go to L.A.," I said.

"L.A.? What for?"

To get money to escape, I thought. "We like you a lot. We like you a lot."

"We have business there, that's what for," I said.

"*Business?* Is Gerda with you?"

"No. And don't tell her. She doesn't know."

"Are you going on the bus?"

I nodded, then said, "Yes." Kristin sure was a snoop! I was beginning to wish I hadn't even called her. "I just wanted to tell you that we wouldn't be going for the crystals, that's all."

"L.A.'s really big," Kristin said. "My dad says it's a jungle. Are you sure you can get wherever you're going? I mean, you don't even know . . ."

"I can get where I'm going and . . ." I swung around, facing the road outside. Now I could see through the glass wall of Henry's office. "Oh, no!" I said.

"What? What's the matter?"

"We've missed the bus, that's what's the matter," I said furiously. "It's just pulling away from the stop." I felt like slamming down the stupid phone. What a great way to start the day! Why had I bothered to call her anyway? Why had I talked so long? Why was I yelling at her?

"Matt?" Kristin's voice was anxious.

I covered Fernando's smiling face with the flat of my hand. "Yes?"

"Nothing," Kristin said and hung up the phone.

Henry and Ab were at the gum machine when I went back outside.

"Why didn't you call me?" I asked Henry. "We missed the bus."

He shrugged. "Seemed like you were in the middle of an important call. Anyway, there'll be another bus in an hour. Relax, Matt."

"A whole hour wasted," I said pulling out the timetable to check, though I knew he was right. *Depart Sierra Maria Canyon, 10:10* A.M.

Henry went on giving Ab more pennies. I swear, he was spoiling her useless.

"Relax," he said again, glancing over at me. "You'll live longer."

I decided that if relaxing had anything to do with living longer, Henry would make it to a hundred and ten.

I gritted my teeth and walked to the front to watch for the next bus. So what if it wouldn't be here for a whole hour. I kept checking the time, walking up and down, warning Ab to be ready to come when I said the word.

It was 10:00 when I saw someone on a too-small bicycle pedaling fast from the direction we'd already come. Kristin!

She came to her skidding stop beside me and pulled off her mashed-up white hat. "Good," she said. "I made it in time."

"In time for what?" I asked suspiciously.

She smiled. "In time to go with you."

13

I TRIED TO argue. "This hasn't anything to do with you, Kristin."

"You're on the trail of Harriette and Isadora, aren't you?" she asked, squinting up at me from her seat on the bicycle.

I held out the portfolio. "We're going to Mr. Stengel's gallery. I'm hoping he'll buy these. I'm not on anybody's trail."

Kristin tapped the bicycle pedal with her foot, spinning it in a blur of silver. "Well, since I'm here, I might as well go along. Mom and Dad and Fee are at a swap meet in Glendale. They're going to lunch at McDonald's after. So . . ." she shrugged.

"Look," I said. "It'll be boring for you."

"Uh-uh. And I can help you find Mr. Stengel's place. I mean, I know my way around. And I can help you get a good price. Since I started selling crystals, I'm a terrific bargainer. Sometimes I can get people to come up, oh, maybe five dollars more than they offered to begin with."

"Wow," I said. "A whole five dollars."

"You don't have to be sarcastic," Kristin said coldly.

"Sorry."

Ab came running over then. "Hi, Kristin. How come you're here?"

"I'm going, too," Kristin said, and Ab said, "Goody. Can we go look for crystals tomorrow, then?"

"We'll see," Kristin told her, and then I spotted the bus coming and I grabbed Ab's hand. "Come on. We don't want to miss this one, too."

Kristin dropped her bike right there, wheels spinning. "Keep an eye on this for me, O.K., Henry?" she yelled.

"Be careful," Henry called after us. "Got your map, Matt?"

"Yeah." I patted my back pocket, and wanted to add: And now we've got Kristin, too. Kristin who knows everything.

Except that pretty soon I discovered she didn't know a thing, either about riding on a bus or getting to L.A. She didn't know you had to have the correct money for the driver. She'd never thought about having to change buses, or needing a transfer.

"You've never ridden a bus before, have you?" I asked.

"Yes, I have. I rode the school bus for two years."

Oh, brother, I thought. Big deal. But I knew better than to say it.

"So how do we know where to get off this one and where to get the other one?" she asked. If I hadn't known better, I might have thought Kristin sounded nervous.

I pointed to the map. "We get off here, at Broadway and First. Then we take the Number 3, north, to Sunset and La Cienega.

"Oh. But how do you *know* that?"

"I read the map and the timetable," I said casually, and I saw something on her face that I'd never seen before. Kristin was impressed! I could hardly believe it. She was impressed with me! Hey, I thought, she's just a little canyon mouse. And I couldn't help grinning.

"What are you grinning for?" she asked suspiciously.

"Nothing," I said, and I decided I was glad she'd come after all. "I took buses a lot in Seattle," I said comfortingly. "You get to know how to do it."

We did it well, and when we finally got off at Sunset and La Cienega, I figured we only had four blocks to walk.

It was still only 11:30, though, and I couldn't see Mr. Stengel till 12. We walked slowly along a street that was lined with galleries till we came to the Black Orchid.

"We're too early," I said.

The gallery right next to it had BLAKELY: FINE ART in antique-looking gold print across the window.

I stood looking at the sign. "Why not?" I asked out loud. "We don't have to sell the paintings if we don't want to, but I wouldn't mind seeing what they'd offer for them in here. Do you want to come in, too, Kristin?" I frowned discouragingly.

"Sure," Kristin said. Kristin definitely was not easily discouraged and I had a feeling she'd already forgotten that she'd never have made it this far without me. I pushed open the heavy glass doors, easing the precious portfolio through.

We were standing in a large bare room that had polished wood floors and a single black line drawing on each of its white walls.

Ab pointed. "That one's nice."

Immediately a tall, thin man standing at the back came toward us. "You have good taste, young lady," he said. "That's Hokusai."

"I like these, too." Ab was looking at three paintings of stick people and a stick dog and a house with smoke coming out of its chimney. She would like those! They were exactly the kind of drawings she always did herself.

"They're neat," Kristin said.

The man turned and his face softened. "Yes. But those are not for sale. They're too valuable. By the way, let me introduce myself. I'm Kevin Blakely. My partner Phoebe and I own the gallery. Is there something else I can show you?"

"Actually, we have some very nice paintings we'd

139

like to show you," I said and held up the portfolio.

"They're even prettier than Mr. Hokey whatever," Abby said, and the man grinned.

"Well, in that case, I'd better not pass on seeing them. Come this way."

The three of us followed him into a little cluttered back studio office and I took Mom's paintings out of the portfolio and placed them carefully on the desk.

Mr. Blakely began going through them, holding them delicately by their edges, examining them slowly at first, then going faster and faster. When he'd seen them all, he put them back in a neat pile and smoothed his hair, though it didn't need smoothing.

"Um," he said. "Yes. Very nice." Before I could ask him *how* nice and if he'd be interested in buying some of them, he said to Abby: "I have chocolate cookies. Would you like one?"

"Oh, yes, please," Abby said.

He took a package from a drawer.

"About the paintings," I began, but he was too busy with the cookie package to talk to me.

"You can just tear it," Abby told him, hopping impatiently from one foot to the other. I swear I'm going to have to do something about Ab. She's getting to be a real greedy little kid.

Mr. Blakely gave her the whole package.

"You want me to do it for you, Abby?" Kristin asked and Abby passed it over.

"So, do you like the paintings?" I asked.

"As I said, they're nice," he told me. "But they're

frankly not our style. We go in for more classical work—woodcuts, prints, etchings, that kind of thing. If you want to sell them, you might try the Art Mart, two streets over."

I raised my eyebrows. "The Art Mart? It doesn't sound too great."

"They do handle more . . . well, more popular stuff."

"Mom made the pictures," Ab said, her mouth filled with cookie. "She died." Ab's eyes can go from happy to sad in the space of a second. "Matt and I look after ourselves now. There's just us. And Aunt Gerda."

"Oh." Mr. Blakely looked from Ab to me and then to Kristin.

"Kristin's our friend," Abby explained.

Mr. Blakely said, "I see," then tapped his fingers on the desk and began sorting through the paintings again. He pulled out one of a garden filled with daffodils that Mom had done last spring. I remembered the day. "This one is pretty," he said. "I could give you . . . oh, fifty dollars."

"Wowee!" Abby said, smiling happily up at me. "Fifty dollars, Matt."

"It's worth a lot more," Kristin said quickly. "Sixty at least."

I slid the paintings back in the portfolio. "Thanks. But I don't think we're desperate to sell. Let's go."

Abby started to protest, but I grabbed her shoulder and nudged her ahead of me toward the outside gallery and the door to the street. Kristin and Mr. Blakely followed behind us.

"I'm sorry I can't do better," Mr. Blakely said.

Abby stopped and pointed to the three stick paintings. "I could make you another one like this," she offered. "And then if you wanted, you could buy it for fifty dollars."

Mr. Blakely smiled down at her. Adults always smile at Ab. "My little boy sent those to me. He lives with his mother in Montreal. I don't see him very often."

"Is that why they're so valuable?" Abby asked.

"That's why." He spoke to me. "If you want to change your mind later, Matthew, and let me have the daffodil . . ."

I interrupted. "That's O.K. But thanks for looking at them." I was wondering if he'd have offered to buy any of them if Ab hadn't spilled that Mom had done them and that she'd died. Did that mean the paintings weren't any good? Naw. It was just that they weren't his style.

I pushed open the door and held it with my back so Kristin and Abby could come through.

"It's not that the paintings aren't any good," I told Kristin. "It's just that they aren't his style. That's what he said."

Kristin nodded.

I wished she wasn't with us.

"It's five minutes to twelve," I added. "We'd better hurry."

The Black Orchid Gallery was a lot bigger and grander than the Blakely gallery. Mr. Stengel's big square showroom had an all-white floor and white walls with strange, modern paintings, pale and transparent, on the walls. I decided standing in here was like standing inside an ice cube.

A woman with silver hair and big, flat silver earrings came out from the back.

"Hello," she said, smiling mostly at Ab, but at Kristin and me, too.

"Hi," I said. "I called yesterday. Mr. Stengel gave me his card." I fished it out.

"Oh, yes. I'm sorry, but he isn't in yet. Would you like to wait?"

"Please," I said.

She stood for a minute, then she said: "Unfortunately, I'm interviewing this morning for a new part-time secretary to help me out, so my office is a bit chaotic. Never mind. I'm sure it will be perfectly all right for you to wait in Mr. Stengel's room."

She led us through an outer office, where a young man was typing so hard he didn't even glance up and where two women sat in black leather chairs, leafing through magazines and looking nervous.

"Here you are." She opened an inside door and motioned toward a gigantic white couch, then said, lowering her voice, "I hope you don't have to wait *too* long. But Mr. Stengel is a bit of a Tom Tardy."

"We can wait," I said.

Mr. Stengel's room was white as the gallery, except

143

that here the floor was covered with carpet, thick and pure as new snow. There was a big dark red desk with a phone on it, and a dark red phone book and a golden clock. Behind the desk was an oversized leather chair. I tried to imagine little Mr. Stengel sitting there. He'd be lost.

There were more pictures on these walls and I walked around examining them. There were garden scenes with ladies carrying parasols and one of a field filled with rows of haystacks, rows and rows and rows. I thought they were a bit like Mom's pictures and I decided we might have a good chance here.

We sat for ages. I figured it had to be after noon, way after. Fortunately, Ab still had the package of cookies to keep her happy and Kristin prowled around, looking at the pictures, counting the haystacks in the field, asking me to guess how many, asking me if I'd ever seen a haystack.

I passed the time by picking Ab's crumbs out of the deep white carpet and trying to stay calm. What if Mr. Stengel didn't want the paintings either? What if he said they were nice in that give-away, not interested kind of voice? What then? Then Kristin would feel sorry for me again and I'd hate that.

The door opened and I thought Mr. Stengel had arrived at last. "Finally," Kristin breathed, but it was just his secretary again. She was carrying a pile of ledgers and she walked to a door that I'd already noticed behind Mr. Stengel's big desk. I guess it was kept locked, because she began messing around with a key, trying to get it in the lock, which she couldn't see properly because of the pile of stuff she was carrying. The top ledger began to slip.

I jumped up. "Here." I saved it, took the key from her, opened the door.

"Thanks, honey," she said.

Inside, paintings were stacked against the walls. There were several glass pedestals and a big white statue of a lady holding a mirror. All this I saw in one glance that took the statue in and let it go again. Because there were two other things in the room.

It wasn't possible. How . . . ?

And then Abby's voice chimed up beside me: "Oh, look, Matty. Mr. Stengel has a dolly, too." Behind me Kristin gave a loud, disbelieving gasp.

Nobody needed to tell me that that was the missing Harriette who stood balanced on her pole against the wall, her face shiny clean and smiling above a white draped sheet. Beside her, formless and blank, was Isadora. Upright like this she could have been one of those mummy cases you see in a museum. The two of them—here. We'd found the missing dolls after all.

14

Mr. Stengel's secretary opened a drawer and slid the ledgers inside.

"Don't say anything about the dolls," I whispered to Kristin and I put my fingers to my lips to make sure Ab got the message, too.

"There." The secretary straightened. "Thanks for your help."

"You're welcome. Those are interesting-looking dolls. Where did Mr. Stengel find them?"

"Oh, some elderly lady has a bunch of them. Her husband made them and Mr. Stengel has been trying to get her to sell to him. I guess she finally gave in and sold these two."

I sensed Abby was about to speak and I gripped her arm and squeezed a warning.

"They're genuine folk art," the secretary went on. "According to my boss, they're almost priceless." She stroked Ab's cheek with her finger. "By the way, my

146

name's Itsy, like Itsy Bitsy Spider. Do you know that song?"

Ab glanced at me for permission to answer and when I nodded, she nodded, too.

"It's fun, isn't it?" Itsy asked, and Ab checked with me again before she nodded a second time.

"Where did you say Mr. Stengel got the dolls?" Kristin asked.

"I believe it was somewhere in Los Angeles County. I think he said it was out on the way to Palmdale. They're pretty strange looking, huh?"

"Really!" I said. "Is it O.K. if we still wait for Mr. Stengel?"

Itsy smiled. "Fine. I expect he'll be here any minute."

I steered Ab toward the white couch. As soon as the door closed behind Itsy, she said in a sulky way: "You squeezed too hard, Matt. I wasn't going to say anything."

"Sorry, kiddo," I said.

Kristin leaned against Mr. Stengel's big desk and fanned herself with her hat. "Can you believe this, Matt? What did she mean Gerda sold them? She never did. What a liar Mr. Stengel is."

"Maybe he bought them from somebody else," I said. "Somebody who stole them." I thought for a minute. "Somebody who stole them *for* him, because Mr. Stengel wanted them so much and Aunt Gerda wouldn't sell." Immediately I got a picture of Clay Greeley's cigar box, the fifty-dollar bills piled neatly inside.

"Oh, man!" Kristin sighed. "And we all thought Mr. Stengel was so nice. I even hoped Gerda would *marry* him. He sure had me fooled."

"Is he not nice, Matty?" Ab asked all agog. "*I* thought he was nice."

"I think he fooled all of us," I said. I remembered the way Aunt Gerda had said: "He comes a lot of- tener now that he has this new interest." I'd thought she meant in her. She'd meant in buying the dolls. But he'd fooled her, too. She never would have dreamed he'd take them.

"I'll just bet he was the one all along," Kristin said. "The one trying to force her out of her house and into an old people's home."

"She wouldn't have been able to bring the dolls with her . . ."

"And she'd sell to him," Kristin finished. "What a sleaze ball! And what about Clay Greeley? I know Mr. Stengel always stopped at Clay's stall. He kidded about what a good businessman Clay was. He must have figured out how greedy he was, too. I bet he paid that creep Greeley to do everything. You know, to make life hard for Gerda."

"And in the end to dig up Harriette," I said.

Kristin squeezed her hat in her hands as if she had Clay Greeley by the neck. "How *could* he? A nice lady like Gerda."

"All's fair in business," I reminded her. "Isn't that what Clay said?"

"So what should we do next, Matt?" Kristin asked. "Should we try to steal them back? But how could we get them past Itsy Bitsy Spider?" She nodded in the direction of the outer office.

I turned toward the windowless room where we'd seen the dolls. "And how do we get in there to get them? The door's locked."

"Can we go home now?" Abby asked. "I don't like it here."

"Not yet, Ab." I was looking at the leather phone book on Mr. Stengel's desk. "I've just thought of something," I told Kristin, picking up the directory, leafing through its pages. There were lots of names listed under G, but no Greeley. One number under G was listed with only the initials, C.G.

"Yeah," Kristin breathed.

She stood next to me as I dialed. At the other end the phone rang and rang. At last someone picked it up and a groggy, bad-tempered voice asked: "Yeah?"

"Is Clay there?"

"No, he ain't. And don't call no more. I'm not Clay's answering service and I'm trying to sleep."

The slam of the receiver almost took my ear off.

"Greeley's?" Kristin whispered. I nodded.

Behind us Abby bounced on the couch and chanted: "No more monkeys jumping on the bed. One fell off and broke his head." Abby doesn't stay worried for long, thank goodness.

I hadn't heard the door open. I hadn't heard his

feet on the carpet or seen him because my back was
turned as I talked on the phone. But there was Mr.
Stengel beside us.

"Hello," he said heartily. "Kristin, isn't it? And
you're Gerda's grandson. And this is your little sister."

"Mrs. Yourra's our great-aunt, not our grand-
mother," I muttered, as if it mattered.

"So what brings you here, my friends?"

"You stole her dolls," I said.

I hadn't meant it to come out like that. I'd thought
I'd trap Mr. Stengel, make him admit to what he'd
done, but the words wouldn't stay inside my mouth. I
wished I had them back, safely hidden. Why had I
blurted them out like that? Maybe he had a gun.
Maybe he'd try locking *us* up in that room. But how
could he, with people in the other office? I didn't
know, but I wasn't sure there was anything he
couldn't do.

"My dear boy." His glance flickered to the locked
door, then back to me.

"I saw them." My voice shook. My legs, too. "We
think you got Clay Greeley to steal them for you."

"Clay Greeley?" It was as if he'd never heard the
name in his life. But Clay's number was in his phone
book and that proved something.

Abby came over and pushed her hand into mine.

"Sit down, all of you," Mr. Stengel's voice even had
a smile in it. "We can discuss this matter intelli-
gently."

"We don't want to sit down." I heard the shake in

Kristin's voice, too, and that gave me a sort of courage.

"It's O.K," I said. "We have to find out about this."

Mr. Stengel had already seated himself behind his desk and I noticed how big he looked there, how important. The chair must have been specially made to be higher so he'd seem that way.

Kristin and I sat on the couch with Ab between us. I kept hold of her hand.

"I want to level with you," Mr. Stengel said. "Then perhaps you'll understand why I did what I did. You'll see it was best for your aunt in the long run."

"I'm sure!" I hoped he understood I was being sarcastic, not agreeing.

"And that's why you were so sneaky and pretended to be her friend," Kristin added. I could tell she was trying to help me out and I had to admit I was glad she was here, that it wasn't just Ab and I.

Mr. Stengel was wearing a white suit with a black shirt and there he sat, big and important and calmly smiling. But I decided he wasn't as calm as he pretended to be when he took out a black handkerchief and wiped his brow.

"Your Uncle Joseph was quite a craftsman," he said. "Unfortunately, he was a poor businessman and your aunt was not left in good shape financially. I offered to take one or two of the dolls to help her out, but . . ."

"And she wouldn't, so you stole them," I said. He didn't seem to hear.

"But she said she wouldn't split up her family. So

she wouldn't sell." He spread out his little hands. "Maybe you could help me convince her. I'd take all of the dolls. I'd give her $500 for each one. That would be . . ." —he put his fingers together and stared at the ceiling—". . . thirty-five hundred dollars."

"What about Harriette and Isadora?" Kristin asked.

"Who?"

I pointed to the locked door.

"All right. With another thousand dollars for them she'd have forty-five hundred. She could pay her bills and . . ."

"And she wouldn't have to worry about getting hit by a rock, or having stuff dumped on her dolls, or another fire." I stopped. Better not push this too far. Better pretend we believe him and wait till we got out of here before I started accusing him.

"Weren't you scared you'd burn up all those valuable dolls along with Aunt Gerda when you set the fire?" Kristin asked.

"My dear young lady, I didn't set the fire. And I made sure those boys knew to start it well away from . . ." Mr. Stengel stopped and gave Kristin a smile and me a sly look. "Uh-oh. You almost got me there."

Those boys! Clay and his friends. They'd even set a fire for him.

"And you turned all the canyon people against her," I said angrily, forgetting that I shouldn't accuse him yet.

Ab scrunched back and whispered, "Matty?" I

squeezed her back and took a deep breath. "It's O.K., Ab."

"You made them all think she was crazy," Kristin said. "You're such a creep."

Uh-oh. Now Kristin *had* said too much. I tensed the muscles of my legs, ready to run. I'd lift Ab, shove Kristin ahead of me. But Mr. Stengel was still smiling. Maybe he'd been called a creep a few times before. He smoothed the wood on his desk with delicate fingers. "You have to remember, Gerda brought a lot of that on herself. She couldn't resist having the dolls talk."

I stared at him. "What do you mean, having them talk?"

"Oh, you must have heard them. Old Joseph had them all wired for sound. There are speakers in those bases where the dolls stand. He and Gerda would have them put on plays for the two of them in the evenings, and he made it so they'd say goodnight to her and call her 'Mother.'" Stengel clicked his fingers. "All Gerda has to do is push the play buttons on the recorders she keeps in the trunk by the door. There's one for each doll."

"*That's* what Clay Greeley and the twins heard," Kristin said to me. "No wonder they were scared."

That's what I'd heard, too, and no wonder *I'd* been scared. Relief flooded through me. Tape recorders. Buttons. I remembered the click I'd heard the night they said "We like you. We like Abby, too." And I almost laughed out loud, even though there wasn't much to laugh about except what a wimp I'd been. "I suppose she can change the message anytime she likes?" I asked.

"Of course. Gerda always did the doll voices. She was good at it. There was a time when Joseph even wanted to do a doll opera and take the show on the road. But Gerda had a voice like a sick cat." His grin invited us to mock Aunt Gerda, too, and I realized he thought we'd softened up because we'd been asking questions about the tape recorders and acting interested.

"So, what do you say, my friends?" he asked. "Partners? Remember, it's for Mrs. Yourra. And there'd definitely be something in it for the three of you." He jumped up and came round the desk, small again, down to his normal size. "As a matter of fact, there could be a great deal in it for all of you."

I stood, too, and Abby scrambled up beside me. I wanted to say: "Never!" But there was still the fear, the knowing that we weren't out of here yet.

"You think we'd go in it with you . . . you . . . you thief?" Kristin asked. "You must be crazy." Shut up, Kristin, I thought. Just shut up.

"So? So what do you plan on doing, then, young lady? Going to the police, maybe? Telling Mrs. Yourra? I advise you, don't any of you try to lock horns with me. You won't win."

My heart was thumping and I was really frightened now. Mr. Stengel was small, but all at once I could feel the evil. We had to get away. I headed for the door, pushing Ab ahead of me. "Let's go."

"Wait," Mr. Stengel said.

I froze. What if I looked back and he had a gun pointed at us? What if he said "Go where? You're not going anywhere."

"You forgot something," he said.

I turned. He was holding Mom's portfolio. How could I have forgotten it? I'd been ready to walk out of here and leave it behind.

"I suppose this is why you came," he said, his mouth a tight line, his eyes tight, too. I'd never seen anybody so terrifying.

"You wanted me to look at these paintings. Well, I'll tell you something. I've seen some of this work before and it's worthless."

He opened the buckles before I could guess what he was going to do, and even if I'd known, I don't think I could have moved to stop him. Not then. He had one of the paintings in his hand now, staring at it with an offended look on his face, dropping it on the floor. It fluttered, in slow motion, drifting like an autumn leaf, the colors blending, twisting . . .

"Oh, no!" Abby pressed her fist against her lips.

Mr. Stengel turned the portfolio upside down. The pictures fell and Abby and Kristin ran to scoop them together.

"Why did you have to do that?" Kristin asked. "These belonged to their mother."

Mr. Stengel smiled. "I know."

"You're a horrible man," Ab said fiercely. "Matt and I hate you."

I knelt beside them, helped slide the pictures carefully back inside the portfolio, took Ab's hand. "Let's go," I said again. This time Mr. Stengel didn't call us back.

Itsy looked up at us and smiled as we went through the front office. "Your patience paid off, then."

"Yes."

Abby sniffled and rubbed her eyes.

"What's the matter?" Itsy asked with a frown. "Are you all right?"

"She's fine," I said.

"She will be when we get out of here," Kristin added.

I took a gulp of fresh air when we reached the sidewalk. We were out. Safe. Free. But what now? What should we do? Would the police believe us? And even if they did, what if they came and Stengel had moved the dolls someplace else?

"Can we go home now?" Abby asked.

I nodded. "Yes."

"I vote we find a phone booth and call my dad," Kristin said. "We can tell him to come down here right away and get the dolls, and punch out Stengel and . . ."

"You said he's not home," I reminded her. "Weren't they staying wherever they went till the afternoon? The afternoon could be too late."

We were passing the Blakely gallery now. Through

the big glass front I could see Kevin Blakely with a young woman who was probably Phoebe, his partner. They were talking and laughing and holding coffee mugs. He saw us and waved and I began to wave back. Instead, I pushed open his door.

"Matt?" Kristin asked, but I was already inside.

"Will you help us?" I asked Mr. Blakely.

"If I can. Is something wrong?" He looked hard at me, then turned to his partner. "Phoebe, you can mind the shop for a while, can't you? Come and sit down, kids."

We did. And we told him the whole story.

15

THE FOUR of us went back to the Black Orchid Gallery.

"I've come to see the dolls," Kevin Blakely told Mr. Stengel.

Itsy hovered nervously by the door. "They insisted on walking right in, Mr. Stengel. I'm sorry."

Mr. Stengel didn't rise from his power place behind his desk. "That's all right, Itsy." He dismissed her with a nod of his head. "What dolls are you referring to, Kevin?"

It was Kristin who pointed to the locked door. "He's referring to the ones in there."

"And Aunt Gerda didn't sell them to you either," I said. "You stole them." I felt braver now that Kevin Blakely was with us. Much braver.

"You're not going to say you don't have them, are you?" Kristin asked.

I pointed, too. "Make him open that door, Mr. Blakely. You'll see."

Mr. Stengel rubbed the edge of his desk the way he'd done before. Maybe the feel of it gave him comfort, or courage. He smiled at Kevin Blakely, not bothering to even glance at any of us. "I found the dolls up in Sierra Maria Canyon," he said. "I borrowed them to show to an interested party. If the price on them is right, I believe the owner will be willing to sell the rest. These two were discards."

"That's a lie," I said, getting braver all the time.

Mr. Stengel didn't look at me then either. It was as if everyone in the room except Mr. Blakely was invisible. "I have them more or less on consignment, Kevin. See what you think," he said and unlocked the door. And there was poor, dead Harriette and lumpy Isadora. It was such a relief to see that they were still there, that he hadn't somehow magicked them away.

Mr. Blakely examined the dolls carefully. "Yes," he said. "I remember a dealer discovered some like these in Nevada not so long ago. As I recall, the artist there didn't want to sell either."

"And what a loss that would have been to the world of art." Mr. Stengel shook his head. The holy expression on his face made me want to throw up. Surely Kevin Blakely wouldn't be fooled by this "all-for-art" talk? Please don't be fooled, Mr. Blakely.

"And you took these from her house without her knowledge?" he asked Mr. Stengel.

I butted in. "From her yard. From her property."

"She's an old friend, Kevin," Mr. Stengel said. "She doesn't know what she has here. When she does, I'm sure she'll see reason. Naturally, I wasn't planning on keeping them."

Mr. Blakely looked at him for the longest time, then shook his head and turned to me. "What would you like to do about this, Matthew?"

"I'd like to take them home."

And that's what we did, Kristin and Ab beside Mr. Blakely in the front of his car, me in the back where Harriette and Isadora lay. I touched Harriette's cheek, warm and smooth as silk, and I discovered I wasn't afraid of her at all.

Art people have come from all over to see the dolls, now that we've been on TV and in the papers. A New York City dealer offered $40,000 for Derek alone.

"Derek is not for sale," Aunt Gerda said.

Of course he isn't. Derek's her child. And now Harriette, her dead daughter, is safely at rest again in her backyard grave.

Mrs. Valdoni wrote saying how terrible all this was and were we all right. Knock Knock and Blinky and John sent a letter. They took turns writing the sentences. They all said I was lucky, and they wished they were in California, that nothing fun like this ever happened in Seattle. All it ever did there was rain. Knock Knock didn't even send a joke.

But I kept thinking that though this publicity was nice, we still didn't have any money. We were famous and poor.

And then Kevin Blakely brought out Mr. Corbin Samuelson, a wealthy art patron. Mr. Samuelson said he'd like to offer us an art endowment. The dolls would be left where they were. "Move them and you lose the soul the artist put into them," Mr. Samuelson said. "The house will stay, and I can arrange funds for the permanent upkeep of the dolls. And for your upkeep, too, Mrs. Yourra, as honorary curator."

"What about Matthew and Abigail?" Aunt Gerda asked. "I'm getting old and . . ."

"For Matthew and Abigail also, in perpetuity," Mr. Samuelson said.

Abby stared. "In *what?*"

"It simply means the home will be here for you, too, for both of you, as long as you need it," Mr. Samuelson explained.

"I would, however, like to put the dolls in a temperature-controlled enclosed glass encasement." That's the way Mr. Samuelson talks, as if he has a sock in his mouth.

Aunt Gerda clapped her hands. "The children will love that, I'm sure. They hate the cold."

"Can you believe these canyon people?" Kristin asks me, endlessly. "Now they're trying to say they liked Aunt Gerda and the dolls all the time. It's sickening."

"Sickening!" I raise my eyebrows and shake my head the way she does.

"And where do you think Clay Greeley went?" she asks.

The police are interested in that, too. They've been here, checking things out, questioning everyone about both Clay and Mr. Stengel. I told them Clay left. I know he did, because I saw him go.

It was a couple of days after we found Harriette and Isadora. I was taking Henry's map back and there was Clay Greeley, waiting at the bus stop and carrying a big old duffel bag.

I took the map in to Henry, came back out, and Clay Greeley was still there.

Part of my mind said skip it, leave it alone, everything's finished. But this wasn't finished. You stood up to Mr. Stengel, I told myself. You can do this, too.

I cycled across the road.

Clay Greeley watched me come, standing there with that same grin on his round pumpkin face. He'd had his hair cut even shorter and the sun made a red shadow around his head.

"Going someplace?" I asked.

"That's right."

"On your own?"

His grin widened. "See anybody with me?"

"No. But . . ." I didn't know what else to say. "Will you be coming back?"

The grin disappeared. "Never." He bit off the word

with a snap of his lips. "Would you come back, if you were me?"

"I . . . I guess not," I said and turned away. I was glad he was leaving.

I'd told Kristin that I'd seen him go. Just that. And each time she asks, "Where do you think he went?" I shrug. "Beats me!"

I've never told her either about going to his house on my own and what I found there.

It's funny how I have secrets about Clay Greeley. It's as if I have some kind of understanding of him, an understanding I can't figure out myself.

"And can you imagine, my mom's still sorry for him?" Kristin says. "She thinks Mr. Stengel used him and that Clay was only a kid. *I* think he was a slug."

"Your mom's nuts," I say. But sometimes I imagine Clay Greeley in a clean, quiet place, in a bed with the sheets tucked neatly in. It's easier to think of him like that, and I'm not sure I want the police to find him.

The twins, of course, say they know nothing about stealing dolls and that they wouldn't go near those dolls if they were paid for it. I think they were paid and they went. But there's no way to prove it.

Aunt Gerda tried to keep Mr. Stengel out of it, for old times' sake, but she couldn't. He's big news. I guess he's going somewhere, too, because Mr. Blakely read in a posh art magazine that the Black Orchid Gallery is up for sale. He told me that the Art Dealers Association of California had sent a letter to all its members saying that Mr. Stengel is no longer connected with them. That means they threw him out.

Mr. Blakely says Mr. Stengel's finished as a dealer. The association will never give him references and without references he won't be able to open a new gallery. As far as I'm concerned, it serves him right and the punishment is not half bad enough. Kristin says he should be locked up for life. I think so, too, and maybe the police will get him even though Aunt Gerda won't press charges.

"I don't think Harold Stengel would ever have taken any of my living children, Matthew," she says.

Not half he wouldn't.

It's almost the end of summer now. Aunt Gerda and I sit out on the porch a lot at night, when Ab's gone to bed. We talk quietly. Behind their partly finished glass walls the dolls listen and smile.

"Have you ever wondered, Matthew, what people mean by valuable?" Aunt Gerda asks me one night. The cold is beginning to creep in and the trees along the canyon road are tinged with orange and yellow. The crickets have disappeared.

I have wondered about valuable a lot. Mom's paintings line my room now, and Abby's room, too. There are some on every wall of the house. Once I'd hoped we'd have an exhibit of her work. We have one. Here. And it's as if she's still with us.

Aunt Gerda rocks peacefully. "Do those people

think the children mean more to me now that I've discovered they're worth a lot of money? Am I supposed to love them more? How foolish."

I know she's speaking about Mom's paintings, too, and trying to comfort me, but I don't need comfort. I began to understand the day I saw the pictures in the Blakely gallery, the pictures that were priceless because they were done by someone Kevin Blakely loved.

I stretch my hand out and Aunt Gerda takes it and we rock peacefully together. It's nice here with her.

Pretty soon she goes in and makes the hot chocolate and I sit, smelling the cool night smells. There's no need to be afraid for our future anymore. No need to be afraid of anything.

And then, from behind one of the half walls of shining glass I hear a faint little voice:

"All's well that ends well, Matthew."

I stop rocking, stare unbelievingly at the dolls, then quickly over my shoulder. Aunt Gerda is carrying a pan of milk to the stove. She must have switched on a tape as she passed. I hadn't heard the click, though.

One of the dolls begins to sing an old-fashioned warble of a song, true and sweet:

"For he's a jolly good fellow . . ."

Another one joins in, and another, singing as softly as bells chiming:

> "For he's a jolly good fellow,
> And so say all of us."

Hadn't Mr. Stengel said Aunt Gerda couldn't sing? He must have made a mistake.

> "For he's a jolly good fellow,
> For he's a jolly good fellow . . ."

I could go in, look at the tapes, check that they're moving, but I don't. Maybe I don't want to know. Or maybe I know already. Instead I just sit back in my chair and enjoy the singing.